"Are my kisses so unwelcome?" he murmured

"They're an unnecessary complication." Her tongue tripped clumsily over the words.

"There's nothing complicated about a kiss."

"Depends who's giving it. Who's receiving it."

"I'm giving," he whispered, "you're receiving...." He kissed her full on the lips, his mouth covering hers with a decisive passion that overwhelmed her defences.

She had not been kissed like that since she was eighteen years old. Not since that night in the summerh

MADELEINE KER is a self-described "compulsive writer." In fact, Madeleine has been known to deliver six romances in less than a year. She is married and lives in Spain.

Books by Madeleine Ker

HARLEQUIN PRESENTS
1138—JUDGEMENT
1161—TAKEOVER
1185—STORMY ATTRACTION
1249—TUSCAN ENCOUNTER
1274—A SPECIAL ARRANGEMENT
1361—TIGER'S EYE

HARLEQUIN ROMANCE
2595—VOYAGE OF THE MISTRAL
2636—THE STREET OF THE FOUNTAIN
2709—ICE PRINCESS
2716—HOSTAGE
3017—TROUBLEMAKER
3063—PASSION'S FAR SHORE
3094—DUEL OF PASSION

MADELEINE KER

KER

Whirlpool

Harlequin Books

TORONTO • NEW YORK • LONDON
AMSTERDAM • PARIS • SYDNEY • HAMBURG
STOCKHOLM • ATHENS • TOKYO • MILAN
MADRID • WARSAW • BUDAPEST • AUCKLAND

Harlequin Presents first edition September 1993
ISBN 0-373-11590-3

Original hardcover edition published in 1992
by Mills & Boon Limited

WHIRLPOOL

Printed in U.S.A.

CHAPTER ONE

'READY, my love?' Caroline Langton poked her head round Kirby's bedroom door. 'Gosh, you look ravishing!'

Kirby Waterford smiled. A pretty, willowy woman in her forties, Caroline was the undisputed leader of Braythorpe society. She had been widowed some five years ago, in the same way as Kirby, through a motor accident. Her husband had left her extremely wealthy. She had never re-married and, indeed, used her widow's status as a kind of lure to maintain a coterie of orbiting males.

During Keith's lifetime, Caroline had been only a passing acquaintance of the Waterfords. But she was a compassionate and loving woman, and since Kirby's own tragedy, a bare ten months earlier, she had been kindness itself.

Kirby, in her turn, had been increasingly drawn to the older and wiser woman, who understood so exactly what she was going through. They were becoming close friends, and, though Kirby did no entertaining these days, invitations to Caroline Langton's farmhouse were a regular occurrence. Weekends spent at Langton Farm— as this one was going to be—meant a great deal to her; they got her out of herself, away from the Lodge and its sad memories...

'There are some people coming tonight whom I really want you to meet,' Caroline told Kirby confidentially, linking her arm through Kirby's as they walked downstairs together. 'Exciting people.' She glanced at Kirby's face. 'Now, don't pull that face. You know that you have to start meeting new people.'

'I know,' Kirby sighed. 'I'm just a little tense tonight.'

'Why?'

'Oh, trouble at the factory. Ever since Keith died, we've had nothing but problems...'

Caroline's eyes were concerned. 'Poor love,' she sighed. 'You shouldn't have all these worries. Why Keith had to saddle you with that wretched factory, I'll never know.'

'Keith didn't expect to die at forty-two,' Kirby grimaced. 'Anyway, I'll tell you about it later, not now. I thought you said this was a party?'

'So it is,' Caroline smiled. 'Tonight is for forgetting your troubles.' They walked into the brightly lit drawing-room. It looked lovely, with a fire roaring in the grate, flowers everywhere, and the drinks trolley waiting hospitably for the guests. There seemed to be an awful lot of glasses, Kirby thought with a twinge. She loved Caroline's company, but ten months after Keith's death she was still terribly unsure of herself in big gatherings.

Of course, Caroline's approach—the sooner she got her life together, the better for her—was logical. It was just a very painful route to take.

Caroline poured them both a glass of champagne, and they toasted one another with a smile, sharing the intimacy of two women who had both known bereavement. They had a lot in common.

'Here's to a good time tonight,' Caroline said.

'To a good time,' Kirby agreed, smiling. The smile lightened the sadness that still haunted her velvet-brown eyes. Not conventionally beautiful, Kirby Waterford had the kind of face that most men found hard to forget, just as they found it hard to ignore the charm of her presence. She had a full, soft mouth to match the gentle eyes; her oval face, framed with dark, curly, lustrous hair, was poised on a slender neck, usually at a quizzical, almost challenging angle.

Tonight she was wearing an evening dress of ruched green silk, in a shimmering emerald shade that did justice to her colouring. The neckline was modestly high, but it plunged rather daringly at the back to show an expanse of Kirby's admittedly excellent figure. She did not have the angular height of a fashion model, but, as so often happened with petite women, her clothes always sat on her beautifully because of her very compactness.

Guests were starting to arrive, and a party of four people in elegant evening dress were being ushered into the brightly lit drawing-room. 'And here,' Caroline said with satisfaction, 'are the very people I want you to meet. Come along, darling.'

She took Kirby's arm and stepped forward, not noticing that Kirby was rooted to the spot, and almost spilling her glass of champagne as a result.

'Kirby,' she protested, 'wake up, darling. Kirby?' She peered at her friend with quick concern. 'Kirby, what is it?'

Kirby was white and motionless. Of the four people who'd just come in, three were perfect strangers. But the fourth needed no introduction.

It had been a long time. A long time since she had last seen Damian Holt. An even longer time since their paths had diverged irrevocably, once and for all.

There was a blaze of recognition in the slate-blue eyes, a moment of stillness that had told her Damian had no more expected to see her here than she had expected to see him.

Then he moved forward, eyes hiding whatever emotion had been in them. 'Kirby! It's been years. How are you?'

Her throat was too tight to reply. As with many very handsome men, the years were dealing more than kindly with Damian Holt. He was bronzed and tough-looking, getting more devastatingly attractive than ever as he reached his later thirties, and he possessed an impact that no woman could ever be indifferent to. Kirby's heart swooped like a kite inside her as she felt his warm fingers close around her own.

Caroline Langton was staring at Kirby's strained face in puzzled concern. 'I had no idea you two knew one another.'

'We're related, as a matter of fact,' Damian said easily, his voice deep-timbred. 'Distant cousins. But we haven't met for three years. Or has it been four?'

'I haven't been counting,' Kirby said, finding her voice at last. With a poise she could never have mustered in the old days, she disengaged her hand from his warm grasp, and forced herself to meet his eyes. 'You look prosperous, Damian. London evidently agrees with you.'

'It does.' Damian's piercing eyes were assessing Kirby with deliberate curiosity. 'The last time we met was at Grace's wedding, wasn't it?'

'I suppose so,' she replied tautly.

He weighed up her face, her rapier-taut poise. 'Four years have made a big difference to you.'

'Not to you. You haven't changed at all.' She put a biting, deliberate emphasis on the words.

'But then, I take pride in not changing,' he replied with a smile. 'Did you expect otherwise?'

Kirby felt the old pain flicker along her veins. So he imagined she was still swooning over him! 'No,' she said. 'I didn't expect otherwise.'

Damian glanced around the room. 'Where's Keith, by the way? I'd like to say hello to him.'

Kirby felt as though a knife had been twisted into her heart. 'You haven't heard, then,' she said in a strained voice.

Damian frowned. 'Heard what? Has something happened to Keith?'

It was Caroline who answered for Kirby, who seemed unable to answer him. 'Keith is dead, Damian,' she explained gently. 'He was killed in a car crash earlier this year.'

Damian's face lost all expression, and Kirby saw the colour of his eyes visibly darken. A stranger might barely have noticed; it was only because she knew Damian's face better than any other human being's that she felt the depth of his shock. For a moment he seemed frozen. 'I didn't know,' he said, very softly. His eyes made them the only two people in the universe, and she felt herself sway. 'Please forgive my blundering stupidity.'

'There's nothing to forgive. How were you to know? I didn't put notices in the London papers. Only in the Yorkshire ones.'

'You should have told me, Kirby,' he said quietly.

She dropped her eyes from his, and shrugged. 'Perhaps I should have done. I'm sorry. But Keith wasn't really a friend of yours.'

'No. But you were.' He let the words sink in for a moment. 'When did it happen?'

'Ten months ago,' she said. 'On the motorway. A lorry went out of control, and crossed the central reservation. Dozens of cars were involved. Keith was on his way to Manchester, with one of the managers. The other man was driving...' Kirby felt the swelling grief threatening her composure. She forced herself to look up at Damian. 'At least it was very quick. He didn't suffer. They were both killed instantly.'

Damian nodded. He was making none of the conventional noises of sympathy and condolence. But then, Damian Holt was not a conventional man. 'I remember that accident. I didn't pay attention to the names. You seldom do.'

'Not until it's your husband. I saw it on television, as a matter of fact. The early evening news. I didn't even think of Keith, until the police came to the door...' She took a breath that was slightly unsteady. 'However, I'm sure this isn't a suitable topic for a dinner party. We're being very rude to your friend.'

'Yes, I must introduce you to Wendy.' He turned to the woman standing beside him. 'Darling, you've heard me talk about my cousin Kirby? Now you're going to meet her. Wendy, this is Kirby Waterford. Kirby, I want you to meet Wendy Catchpole, my fiancée.'

Kirby heard a roaring in her ears, and she swayed dizzily, her arm brushing Caroline's. Damian's fiancée.

Wendy Catchpole was classically attractive, with a tall and graceful figure. She had wide, rather cold green eyes and long blonde hair. 'Damian has mentioned you, Kirby,' she said with regal condescension. 'You're just as pretty as he said you were.'

Kirby somehow kept her empty smile in place. 'Thank you. Nice to meet you, Wendy. Excuse me, please.'

She turned, and walked away to greet some acquaintances who were just arriving. She knew she was being very rude, but she'd simply had to move, or risk collapsing in a ridiculous faint. Her head was still swimming...

Damian's fiancée.

She could feel Damian's eyes on her back, and heard Caroline murmur something in a low voice, no doubt making the usual excuses: She's not really over it yet...still hates to talk about it...needs time to recover...

She forced herself to smile, shake hands, kiss cheeks, make small talk to friends. The soul, she was thinking, doesn't bear wounds the way the body does. If it did, hers would have been a criss-cross of silvery scars, each one bearing the name of Damian Holt. She'd thought he couldn't hurt her any more, but she'd not bargained for the idea of his marrying...

Right now, her criss-crossing of ancient scars were aching and bleeding in a dozen tender places. Pains she'd thought long-since dormant were awakening into life.

The last time they had met had been at a wedding, in London, not long after her own marriage to Keith. She and Damian were cousins, in a distant way of speaking, and they had both attended Grace's wedding out of family reasons. They had spoken, briefly, during the reception. Just polite how are yous and what have you been doings, nothing significant at all.

She'd had Keith with her then, and his presence at her side had enabled her to cope almost relaxedly with the stress of seeing Damian again. Keith had known a fair bit about her and Damian, and Kirby had almost welcomed the chance to show her new husband just how well she'd got over her crush on her gloriously handsome, brilliant, alluring cousin.

Damian and Keith...

Damian had been her whirlpool. And Keith had been her rock. In that awful black period after Damian had gone out of her life, Keith Waterford had offered her his support, and then his love, and she had clung to both with the undiscerning eagerness of a drowning woman. If only he were here tonight! She was longing for his calm, his support beside her.

But she would never have Keith's support again.

*   *   *

Sitting opposite Damian at Caroline's glittering table during dinner, Kirby felt her nerves twisted to breaking-point, keeping her as tense as a duellist. Damian was talking wittily and easily, as he'd always been able to do. But he wasn't talking to her. She was just there, another of the guests.

John MacIntyre, an elderly man who'd been a friend of Keith's, leaned over to Kirby. 'Kirby, darling, you've been as quiet as a mouse all night. What's this I hear about you wanting to sell the Jaguar?'

'I'd like to change it,' Kirby nodded. 'I'd like to get something much smaller.'

'Why?'

'I think a smaller car suits a single woman better. That's all.'

'You could always get a chauffeur if you don't like driving, you know.'

'That would only be more ostentatious, which is what I'm trying to avoid.'

'But you have a position to maintain, Kirby,' John MacIntyre said. 'The Jaguar is the right sort of car for you.'

'I don't think so,' she replied lightly.

'If I had a Jaguar, I'd never sell it,' Wendy Catchpole commented from the other side of the table, turning her crystalline eyes to Kirby. 'Daddy makes the firm buy him the latest model every year.'

Kirby's oval face remained impassive, though her lids drooped slightly over her velvet-brown eyes. 'I'm sure a Jaguar suits a man in your father's position. It just isn't my style. Not now. It's too big.'

And it reminded her too much of Keith, though she couldn't say that. Every time she got into its leather-scented driving seat, she was reminded of his absence, of the fact that she was in his place. Without him.

Her husband had loved the car. He'd bought it only a few months before his death, but he would have understood her desire now for something smaller and less ostentatious. He would have laughed, and shaken his head. You'll never change, he would have said. Underneath the glamour and the beauty, you'll always be the quiet Yorkshire lass I fell in love with. And in his grey eyes she would have seen the loving indulgence that said, Anything you want, my darling, anything at all.

She suddenly found she was fighting back tears, and cursed her weakness.

'What about you, Damian?' Caroline asked him with a smile. 'Wouldn't a nice big Jag suit your image as a top company director? Or has the devil already bought you a Rolls?'

'With parking the way it is in London,' Damian replied, 'I couldn't run either. Not even with the devil's help. I have a Porsche.'

'What's all this about the devil?' John MacIntyre asked.

'Oh, Damian's in league with the powers of darkness,' Caroline smiled. 'I thought everyone knew that.'

'Good lord!' John said.

'She merely means that I've made a lot of money,' Damian explained drily.

'I mean that you sold your soul to the devil years ago,' she laughed. 'Can you deny it?'

Glancing sideways at Caroline, Damian lifted his wine glass to his smiling lips. 'I suppose not.' He had such beautiful hands, Kirby thought absently. Strong, precise, sensual. The only hands whose touch on her body had ever made her pulses race, and the fever rise in her blood. She fought that thought down painfully.

'Is the devil's pay worth it?' she asked, making one of her few contributions to the conversation.

'I've found that being on his staff pays very hand-somely,' Damian nodded solemnly. His suit, as if to underline the point, was exquisitely cut. The black silk had been tailored to hug, rather than flatter, his broad shoulders and deep chest. A figure like Damian Holt's didn't need flattering. It spoke for itself.

'The Holt Corporation runs dozens of companies, doesn't it?' someone asked. 'It must be very exciting.'

'It can be,' Damian shrugged. 'But you'd be surprised how dull it can get. Business tends to be endless varia-tions on the same few themes. And for the same few motives.'

'What themes?' Caroline asked.

'Greed, envy, spite.' Damian had always possessed a dazzling smile, and he used it now. Beautiful white teeth and glittering, slate-blue eyes. Deep, curving laughter-lines on either side of a mouth that had been chiselled to bewitch foolish women. Strong, high cheekbones that linked through aristocratic temples to a high, broad forehead. Crow's-feet, starting to deepen now that he was past thirty-five, reaching towards the silver wings in the dark hair.

The most attractive man Kirby had ever seen, and ever would see.

'Spite, envy, greed,' his deep voice went on. 'The pursuit of wealth and power, my dear Caroline, by whatever means are closest to hand, no matter how mean or petty or dishonest they may be.'

'And you?' Caroline was leaning her delicate chin on one hand, smiling at Damian dreamily. 'Are you the Robin Hood in this dark Sherwood Forest, robbing the rich to protect the poor?'

'The poor?' Wendy Catchpole smiled prettily. 'Darling Damian is dedicated to seeing that the rich keep on getting richer and richer.'

'Her way of saying I try and meet my responsibilities to my shareholders,' Damian interpreted.

'You had a spot of bother in the Third World recently, didn't you?' The comment had come from one of the men. 'I've been following the Sydenham Chemicals case in the papers.'

'Sydenham Chemicals?' Caroline asked, tilting her head. 'That rings a bell somewhere.'

'Spillage of chemicals in some river, somewhere in the Third World,' John MacIntyre explained laconically. 'Dead fish everywhere. All the environmental groups up in arms. Not to mention the local fishermen, who had an economic disaster on their hands. Their government sued Sydenham Chemicals for several million to pay for the clean-up. Sydenham happens to be owned by the Holt Corporation. Director and owner, Damian Holt.' He turned to Damian, his expression speculative, rather than warm. 'But, by the time Damian Holt had finished with them, they were glad to get a few hundred thousand.'

'Some Robin Hood!' Caroline exclaimed. 'Damian, I'm shocked!'

'Just paying the devil back,' he smiled. 'He likes to get his way.'

'And a few hungry fishermen or a few dead fish here and there don't really matter, do they?' Kirby said, not bothering to veil her irony. She'd read about the incident herself, some weeks ago, and had been disgusted at the time. Right now, she'd been sickened even further by his flippant response. But he was impervious to her barbs. He always had been.

'The devil's wages have the advantage of being generous, and being always paid in advance. All he asks is due repayment...when the time comes.' Damian glanced around the table, the centre, as always, of attention. His eyes were laughing at them all. 'If anyone else here is struggling with his or her conscience, my professional advice is to throw your hand in with His Infernal Majesty as soon as possible. Nobody has yet proved the existence of the human soul, but large figures on one's bank statements are a great comfort. And a few dead fish, as Mrs Waterford says, hardly matter at all.'

Caroline snorted. 'Don't you ever toss any sops to your conscience, Damian? Don't you ever do anything altruistic?'

'It's a very rare phenomenon. You're talking about charitable causes? Donations and aid? Not very promising, I'm afraid.'

'He's only trying to sound more loathsome than he actually is,' Wendy spoke up. 'Actually, the Holt Corporation does its share of charity work. They give away millions in research grants to poor countries. And Damian does one or two other little things. He's not completely unredeemed.'

'Well, I'm relieved to hear it,' Caroline smiled, 'even though I doubt whether a few million here or there makes much difference to the Holt Corporation. I'm going to ring for the pudding, and then we ladies will leave you gentlemen to your port, your cigars, and your tall stories.'

The trifle was being brought in—a magnificent creation in a huge crystal bowl, and the universal 'ahh' of admiration successfully deflected the conversation from Damian's work.

Kirby turned to Damian's fiancée. 'When are you planning to get married?' she heard her own voice ask, almost normally.

'Oh, we haven't set the date yet. Probably some time in the new year, when the pressure of work drops a little.' Her voice was crisp and precise, like the eyes that were assessing Kirby. Wendy Catchpole's skin, like Damian's, was tanned, as though she and Damian had just come back from some sunny holiday, and the long, unfussy sweep of golden hair sat exquisitely on her brown shoulders.

She wore diamonds at her ears and throat, matched by the big diamond engagement ring on her left hand. Rich, upper class and poised, Kirby thought numbly. Exactly the sort of woman Damian would marry.

'I hope you'll be very happy,' Kirby said, somehow making it sound warm.

'Oh, we intend to be.' Was there disdain in those beautiful, glass-green eyes? Had Damian told this Nordic blonde all about what a fool Kirby had made of herself over him, about the absurd and extravagant passion she had once nurtured? Wendy's face gave nothing away. She went on, 'May I offer my condolences, by the way? Your husband's death was very tragic. One doesn't quite know what to say, does one?'

'I'm getting over it,' Kirby said neutrally. 'But thank you. You're not Yorkshire, are you?'

'Oh, no,' the other woman laughed, as though the idea was ludicrous. 'I was born in Hampshire.'

'Of course. How long have you known Damian?'

'Oh, quite some time.' The precise, rather clipped voice exuded self-possession, and Kirby listened in silence as Wendy Catchpole went on talking about herself and Damian, her well-shaped mouth forming each syllable with confident, metallic precision.

She worked in a London financial company of which her father, Gerald Catchpole, was a senior partner.

Daddy was evidently a very wealthy man who'd made large loans to Damian Holt for various projects, and that was how she had first met 'darling Damian'.

They had been going out for some time, although things, as Wendy put it, 'hadn't got serious' until some eighteen months ago.

They'd become engaged during the summer, and, as Kirby had guessed, had just been abroad to Portugal with one another. Wendy Catchpole was obviously extremely proud of her important husband-to-be.

'He's a marvellous person,' she concluded with her bell-like laugh. 'An absolute darling. But then, you know that, don't you?'

'Oh, yes,' Kirby nodded. 'I know that very well indeed.'

She turned away, and spent the rest of the evening in conversation with some rather dull friends of Keith's, studiously avoiding Damian's whirlpool eyes.

Towards midnight, when the majority of Caroline's guests had left, and only the closer friends remained, sitting talking intimately in the glassed-in patio, Kirby felt it was time to take her bruised self to bed.

She heard Wendy Catchpole's rather metallic laugh from the patio. Not wanting to see her or Damian again, or draw attention to her withdrawal, she found Caroline, and said her goodnights.

'I could see you were tired and edgy all evening,' Caroline said compassionately. 'I hope it hasn't been too much of a strain.'

'Don't be silly. It's been a lovely evening.'

'Anyway, you've got the rest of the weekend to relax in. You didn't tell me you and Damian Holt were relations, by the way. I had no idea.'

'Well, we don't keep in touch these days.'

Caroline studied Kirby's face inquisitively. 'You don't like him one little bit, do you?'

'I'll tell you about it some time,' Kirby smiled tightly.

'You should keep in touch with him. He's a useful man to know. He could give you excellent advice about the problems you're having with Waterford Electronics.'

'I'm not planning to ask him,' she said, deadpan.

'A man like Damian can be useful for all sorts of things. Take my advice, Kirby: keep useful men around you. This is a hard world for a woman on her own,' she said with simple and unsentimental frankness. 'Women's liberation is all very well when everybody's being civilised. But when the going gets rough, a woman finds she needs a man on her side, if only to defend her from the other men.'

'I'll bear that in mind,' Kirby said.

They exchanged kisses, and Kirby slipped quietly into the hallway.

On impulse, she decided to find herself something to read in the library. On nights like this, sleep was often an elusive friend, and she sometimes read until dawn, sitting up in bed.

The book-lined, oak-panelled library was softly lit. She started hunting through the shelves. It was not easy to find the kind of thing she wanted, and she examined and rejected several books without success. Then she heard the door open, and felt another presence in the room. She turned, and gave a little gasp as she saw Damian.

His tall figure was in semi-darkness as he leaned in an alcove, watching her.

'I had a feeling you might come in here.'

'Did you? You must have powers of telepathy, as well as everything else,' she replied.

He pulled out a heavy, leather-bound volume, and flicked through it casually. 'You made it very obvious tonight that you share Caroline's disapproval of my progress,' he said, his eyes on the pages.

'Disapproval?' Kirby shook her head slowly. 'No. I think it's more…disillusionment.' She held his eyes. 'You have prodigious talents. You're using them in the service of Mammon. That's sad.'

'The service of Mammon?' he repeated, amused. He slid the book back home into its slot on the crowded shelves. Then he turned to Kirby, wearing a half-smile, and surveyed her. 'You sound like a Calvinist minister.'

'Perhaps I do.'

'Is being wealthy a sin?' he asked. 'In that case, you're not free of taint yourself, are you? You're not exactly starving.' She didn't answer. 'Well,' he shrugged, 'we've both come a long way from our origins, haven't we, Kirby?'

'A long, long way,' she agreed quietly. She looked away from him with an effort, and pretended to be absorbed in her search for a book. 'I wasn't expecting to see you here tonight, Damian.'

'Caroline mentioned something about a charming young widow I ought to meet.' He shrugged one shoulder. 'I didn't associate you with the word, "widow".'

'Oh, yes,' she said bitterly, 'I'm a widow. A rapacious, man-hungry widow. So tell me, Damian, is it really safe for you to be closeted alone in a country house with me?'

'I have Wendy to chaperon me now, haven't I?'

'You don't need a chaperon, Damian. I got over you a long time ago.'

'Then perhaps we can enjoy a more normal relationship. As friends and cousins.'

Her voice stayed calm. 'Yes, of course.' She gave him one of her almost-real smiles. 'Your fiancée is very pretty.'

'I'm glad you approve of *something*,' Damian said easily. 'I think Wendy is the right woman for me.'

Kirby didn't change her expression, even though that had been like a deliberate slap across the face. 'I'm sure you deserve one another. It sounds as though your new father-in-law is going to be equally suitable.'

'So it seems,' he replied non-committally.

'And what are you and Wendy doing back in Yorkshire?'

'Six weeks' holiday. I thought I'd revisit the scenes of my long-lost youth before I entered the bonds of wedlock.' His dark eyes trailed down her figure, assessing the lines of her slim body. 'Marriage has changed you, Kirby,' he said softly, eyes moving back up to her oval face. 'It's made you so much more adult. So much more poised.'

'Has it?' she asked with an indifference that was almost detached. 'And how does widowhood suit me?'

Damian didn't wince. He was too assured a man for that. But it was a moment before he replied. 'I'm very, very sorry about Keith. It was a terrible thing to happen. To you, to him.'

'I've been a widow for ten months, Damian. I'm no longer distraught.'

'No. You have other problems on your plate these days.'

Kirby looked up into the dark blue eyes quickly. 'What do you mean by that?'

'Caroline tells me that Keith left you complete control of Waterford Electronics. Is that right?'

'Yes.'

'That makes you a very rich woman.'

'On paper,' she said tersely, 'yes.'

'And a woman with a lot of responsibilities. I don't think Keith Waterford would have wanted you to have to run his company single-handed after his death,' he went on, watching her closely.

'Perhaps not,' she conceded coolly. 'But things don't always work out, do they?'

'If you ever need any kind of help, I hope you'll have the sense to consult me...'

She looked up at him with a hint of sarcasm in her velvet eyes. 'Thank you. The trouble is—how much would your help cost me?'

He had a way of smiling that didn't move his mouth. The laughter-lines just deepened, and his eyes made your heart miss a beat. 'Time has made you cautious. Once upon a time you were so impulsive.'

'Whereas you were always thinking three moves ahead,' she said drily.

'Caroline was telling me that you've had a lot of problems lately. She thinks that the factory is getting a little too much for you these days.'

'Does she?' Kirby asked coolly, pulling a book out of the shelves. 'I'm afraid that Caroline tends to launch into things without consulting people. I don't want any help, Damian. I'm managing perfectly well.'

'You must find your responsibilities a crushing burden, Kirby.'

'I'm managing,' she repeated, curtly enough to snub him.

'Why haven't you appointed a chairman yet? From what Caroline told me tonight, there's no shortage of applicants for the post.'

'For one simple reason. There's no one I can trust. I don't actually want to talk about it, Damian. I only came in to find a book.' Successfully disguising the effort it took, Kirby turned away from him, and started perusing the shelves.

'Find trouble sleeping?' Damian asked.

'I simply like reading in bed,' she told him with a flash of irritation at his perception.

'I know you still feel bitterness towards me,' Damian said quietly. 'You probably always will. But any time you find you *can't* manage, give me a call. I'll be staying at the Beechings for the next six weeks.'

'Thank you.' She was pretending to look through the travelogue she'd selected, though the print was a blur in front of her eyes.

'I'll get back to the party. Sleep well, Kirby.'

She heard the rustle of his suit as he walked past her. For some reason, she had a panicky instinct that he might touch or kiss her, and she swayed on her feet, her eyes closing. But he did not, and when her mind had cleared she was alone in the library.

Whispering a curse bitterly, she turned and walked up to her single bed.

CHAPTER TWO

KIRBY had loved Damian Holt ever since she could remember. There were so many kinds of love, she knew
that. And she had felt most of them, at one time or
another, for Damian.

Kirby lay in bed, in the darkness, fully awake. Her
mind was flooded with memories of Damian, memories
that she'd kept under lock and key for six long years.

As a child, she had worshipped him unquestioningly,
innocently. Ten years older than the curly-haired little
girl who'd begged to ride on his broad shoulders, Damian
had shown a patience and an affection for his cousin
that went beyond his years. They were actually only dis-
tantly related, but her parents and his had always been
close, linked more by friendship than by the rather
tenuous family connection.

Neither Kirby nor Damian had brothers or sisters.
Living in the name neighbourhood, with parents who
were close, they had seen a great deal of each other as
children.

Or, to be truthful, it had been Kirby, as soon as she
could toddle, who had sought out Damian Holt's
company whenever she could do so. She'd adored
Damian from her earliest years.

Of all the games adults devised for her, she'd loved
Damian's the best. Damian had that wicked sense of fun,
that insight into the way her mind worked, that made
every moment with him a fresh delight. No one had ever
excited her the way Damian had done. No one had ex-
panded her imagination in the same way, not even Mum

and Dad. It was Damian who had brought her books to read, Damian who had taken her to the pantomime and the circus. And then, as she'd entered her teens, to the theatre and concerts.

By that stage, her love for him was deepening into a new phase.

As her womanhood emerged, Damian had become her beau ideal, her pin-up, her heart-throb. No one else could ever match his strength, his looks, his charm. By the time she was fifteen, she'd believed that she would never marry anyone but Damian. She loved him, and their destinies, as far as she was concerned, were inextricably entwined. It was just a question of waiting until she was old enough to be his wife.

In his early twenties, Damian was finishing his business degree at Leeds University—getting the highest marks ever recorded, naturally—and thinking about starting his own company, backed only by his extraordinary brain and business sense.

He'd done exactly that, floating a trading company in Braythorpe, which was still going strong. Damian's brilliance had shone out like a beacon. In two years, he was on his way to becoming a rich man, and had more clients than he could deal with. When she'd left school at seventeen, equipped with basic but thorough secretarial skills, Damian had offered Kirby her first job as a typist in his office.

The next eighteen months had been the happiest period of her life. She'd seen Damian eight hours a day, six days a week, had worked with him, talked to him, lunched with him, been within touching range of him, listening to his voice, feasting her eyes on his face and figure.

Happiest, that was, in a qualified sense.

There had also been a constant pain in Kirby's life, a pain that had haunted her teenage years with increasing frustration.

The pain of Damian Holt's notable success with other women.

There were dozens of them. Mostly of the sophisticated, poised type that made a rather shy adolescent girl feel as insignificant as a dried leaf in the wind. He'd never had a prolonged attachment to any of them; but then, he'd made no secret of the fact that he liked being free and footloose, and that he enjoyed female company—a lot of it.

Why couldn't he see how much it hurt her? Why did he never seem to think of *her* as an adult? He took her out, often, but it wasn't the same. He never took her to nightclubs, for example, never took her to places where grown-ups had fun. He seemed almost unaware of her womanhood at times.

The most agonising moments of all had been when Damian had confided his girlfriend problems to her. As though she weren't involved. As though it wouldn't affect her.

She became determined to show him her womanhood. She'd succeeded in doing that, all right. But, as his awareness grew, it only widened the gulf between them, rather than bridged it. It was an awareness that kept her at arm's length, and meant that the kisses and cuddles, the teasing and intimacy they had shared all their lives, became a thing of the past—even though she had never loved him more than she did now, with every fibre of her woman's heart.

The dreadful thought had started creeping into her mind that maybe it wasn't going to work out the way she'd dreamed. That maybe she wasn't destined to be Damian's wife, after all.

Kirby Bryant had drawn her share of attentive males. By eighteen, she'd developed beauty, and an alluringly feminine figure, and men automatically seemed to love her. Men other than Damian, that was. If she'd really wanted to go to nightclubs and dance-halls, there were queues of boys ready to take her. But that wasn't what she wanted. She just wanted to be with Damian. Anywhere. Any time. Always.

Until that day. Her eighteenth birthday. The day Damian had chosen to shatter all her dreams.

She didn't want to think about that, not now.

Kirby sat up in bed, putting the light on, and reached for the travelogue she'd picked out in the library downstairs. She had little interest in the text or the vivid pictures, but anything was better than the misery of her own thoughts right now. Anything to stop her thinking about Damian Holt, and his poised, beautiful fiancée.

She awoke the next morning with the book still in her lap, feeling tired and depressed. But a lively breakfast with Caroline soon cheered her up, and they spent a happy Saturday in one another's company, doing some idle shopping in the morning, and in the afternoon going for a long walk across the grounds of Langton Farm, in the company of Caroline's six assorted dogs. Although Caroline was never one to invite confidences, Kirby always found it easy to talk to her, not just about her loneliness, but about the problems brewing at the factory.

There was one rebuke, however, she felt she had to deliver.

'I know you were being your usual kind self, but I really wish you hadn't said anything to Damian Holt about me or my problems.'

Caroline stopped dead to blink at her friend. 'Why on earth not? He seems quite willing to help——'

'He isn't the person I would have chosen to confide my troubles in.'

'Have you something against him? Because you think he's too ruthless—that business about the pollution clean-up claim?'

Kirby smiled tightly. 'Oh, Damian's been involved with uglier cases than that. When you said he'd sold his soul to the devil, you were closer to the truth than you thought.'

'Business is a very hard environment. A company director has to protect his shareholders from loss,' Caroline said in a gentle voice. 'It doesn't mean he's altogether corrupt.'

'I know. But, in any case, my reasons are more personal. He and I were once... rather closer than we are now.'

Caroline Langton's expression became concerned. 'Darling, I seem to keep putting my foot in it. I won't ask what's between you, but you *were* Keith's wife for five years, so it must be well in the past by now.'

'It is,' Kirby said quietly.

'Then don't be too diffident. He's the *perfect* man to advise you, and his being a relation is all the better. At least talk to him about the factory while he's here in Yorkshire. Tell him the outline, anyway. He'll give you the very best counsel.'

Kirby's normally sweet features tightened. 'I don't want to get entangled with him in any way at all. And I doubt whether he feels he owes *me* anything, either.'

'Old lovers,' Caroline smiled, stooping to toss a stick for one of the dogs, 'generally make very good advisers. In my experience, at least. Never mind him owing you anything, Kirby. Let him help, if he's willing to.' She gave her friend a quick sideways glance from under her fringed scarf. 'So. You and the great Damian Holt. I must say I approve of your taste! He's one of the most gorgeous men I've ever come across. I met him earlier this year, in London, and I was quite bowled over by him.'

'Yes. He tends to cut a swath.' They walked off the path, down into a rough pasture. The vast sky above them was a mackerel patchwork of clear blue and grey cloud, the wind flattening the grass and bracken like the rough smoothing of an invisible giant's hand. The dogs, having scented a rabbit, were arrowing across the field, baying, howling or yapping according to breed.

'He's very different from Keith.' Caroline was watching the dogs with thoughtful blue eyes. 'Not that Keith wasn't a marvellous person in almost every way. But Damian Holt is a different kettle of fish.' She didn't elaborate on that. 'You must have been very young when you knew him.'

'We stopped seeing each other when I was eighteen,' Kirby answered tersely.

'And you married Keith at nineteen,' Caroline commented. 'What did you think of Wendy Catchpole, that fiancée of his?' she asked, almost inconsequentially.

'She struck me as the perfect choice for him,' Kirby said steadily.

'Did she? I thought just the opposite.'

'Well, she's obviously wealthy, intelligent and self-confident,' Kirby replied, 'all things that Damian admires. She's also very beautiful, and I thought she was quite charming last night. Why do you think she isn't suitable?'

'Because she's not special.' Caroline shrugged and smiled. 'Don't ask me to explain myself, because I can't. But Damian Holt is special, and she is not, for all her looks and money. She may even be clever, as you say, though I'm no judge of that, being a dunce myself. But she's not clever enough to hold his interest for long. If they do get married, it won't last. He needs someone special, as special as he is.'

Kirby smiled. 'So what exactly are the criteria for being *special*, Caroline?'

'I told you, I don't know. Some people just are special. Like Damian. Like you.' She turned to whistle for the dogs, and they came panting back, tongues hanging rather shamefacedly at not having caught their rabbit. 'Let's get back and have some tea. I'm frozen.'

'So am I.' Kirby was silent, lost in thought as they walked back to the farmhouse, her soft mouth down-turned at the corners.

'I've asked them to come riding tomorrow,' Caroline remarked casually as they reached the house.

'Who?'

'Damian and Wendy. I thought the four of us might take the horses out across the dale if it's fine, and have lunch in one of the village pubs. If not, we'll try the dubious attractions of a hack along the lane, where it's more sheltered.'

Kirby's heart sank into her shoes. She gave her friend an old-fashioned look. 'Caroline!'

'Don't look like that. The horses need the exercise. It isn't all that often we get four people under sixty in this house!' Her eyes were sparkling as she took Kirby's arm. 'Come on. Hot buttered scones are calling.'

As it turned out, Sunday was a fine autumn day, windy and far from warm, but with few clouds in the sky, and an invigorating tang in the air. Damian and Wendy arrived before lunch, Damian in denims and an old outdoor jacket, the same sort of outfit that Kirby herself was wearing, and Wendy in expensive and elegant riding gear that looked as though it had never been used.

Kirby had been dreading the afternoon, and her tension made her even more curt and hostile towards Damian than on Friday night. She could hardly wait to get mounted, and release some of her depression in exercise.

Caroline's horses were fine animals, though none got much exercise these days. They were strong, enthusiastic mounts, and the ride, down from the farm through Braydale, named after the river Bray that eventually ran through Braythorpe town, was upliftingly beautiful.

Despite her comments about Wendy Catchpole yesterday, Caroline was obviously making an effort to be pleasant to the girl this afternoon, and rode at her side, encouraging her to talk about her background, her career, and her general likes and dislikes.

Riding a little ahead, Damian and Kirby were far less talkative—Kirby especially silent, since riding out with Damian brought back memories of other rides, long ago. They weren't memories she wanted or welcomed. Any conversation they had was stilted and formal.

'The air's so clean and pure out here,' Damian sighed in satisfaction. 'London air always smells of traffic. I miss the country.'

'Yes. You always were one for the simple life,' Kirby commented sweetly.

They crossed the river, rode along a quiet B-road for a mile or so, and then cut across open moorland towards the pretty little Dales village of Wetherton.

The uncluttered horizon gave Kirby a sudden need to spread her wings. She urged her horse into a brisk canter, determined to leave some cobwebs behind her. Damian kept pace with her, a dark figure on a dark horse a few yards to her side. Half wanting to shake him off, half wanting to challenge him, she allowed the canter to turn into a gallop.

It wasn't the most sensible thing to do, as the dense purple heather made it impossible to see any holes or obstacles in her path, but Kirby was drinking in the exhilaration, revelling in the feel of the wind in her hair and the surging horse between her thighs as they picked up speed.

Damian, riding the big bay, easily outpaced her, and she found herself chasing him, spurred on by the mocking grin he flashed her over his shoulder. Careering down the hillside, she felt the blood coursing in her veins, sparkling like champagne. The rush of the wind, the drumming of hoofs, filled her senses. Eventually, the grim line of a drystone wall brought their headlong rush to a halt, but she was laughing with sheer pleasure as she reined back beside Damian, her horse blowing and snorting as though it had relished that sprint as much as its rider.

'Bee get under your saddle?' he enquired in amusement.

She twisted to look back over her shoulder, and realised that she was alone with Damian in rather a lot of North Yorkshire. Wendy and Caroline, keeping their sedate pace, were almost half a mile behind them, two dots against the glorious grey and purple of the hillside.

'We'd better wait for the others,' she panted.

'Yes,' he agreed. 'Wendy isn't all that good a horsewoman.'

'What, with that beautiful outfit?' Kirby couldn't help asking maliciously. Her oval face was flushed, her hair in a chestnut tangle. She sent Damian an ironic glance from bright brown eyes. 'You ought to be at her side, then, in case she falls off. Or something.'

'She won't fall off at that pace.' He was watching Kirby with those dark blue eyes. Under this big autumn sky, they had taken on an ultramarine glow that made Kirby's heart lurch inside her breast. 'You look as though you needed that gallop,' he said.

'I did.' She leaned forward to pat her mount's sweaty neck in approval. 'I don't get to ride a horse all that often these days.'

'Why not?'

'Oh…various reasons. Like not having anyone to ride with.'

'You should think about remarrying,' he said calmly. They were walking the horses along the wall, sheltered from the wind in its lee.

She flashed a glance at him. 'Just in order to get a riding companion? No, thanks.'

'There are other reasons for marrying.'

'How would you know?' she asked pointedly. 'You've never tried it. I have.'

'True,' he admitted. His lean, strong body moved in the saddle with the grace of poetry. 'I don't need to ask whether your marriage to Keith was happy.'

'No,' she replied with off-putting curtness, 'you don't.'

'But I will, anyway.' His teeth glinted whitely in a quick smile. 'Was it happy?'

'Blissfully happy,' she said shortly. 'Keith was a wonderful husband.'

'So you can recommend marriage as an institution?'

She knew he was laughing at her. 'Providing you choose the right partner,' she said stiffly. 'And you seem pretty sure you've done that.'

'Pretty sure,' he repeated. He was riding on the outside, still watching her. 'You'll be twenty-five this December, won't you?'

She nodded. 'Quite an old lady,' she said with a dry smile.

'Wait until you reach *thirty*-five.' His deep voice was husky. 'As a matter of fact, you're far more lovely now than you were at eighteen.'

Kirby's face tightened. 'Compliments, Damian? I think it's a little late in the day for that.'

'The simple truth,' he corrected her. 'There isn't a line on your face, yet so much about you has changed. Become maturer. Colder.'

'Colder?'

'That's an essential component of beauty, don't you think? Mere prettiness is warm. True beauty is always cold.' They had reached a little wooden gate, where they stopped. Kirby glanced at him warily. Damian's eyes were penetrating. 'You're also filled with bitterness, Kirby. Has widowhood done that to you? Or was it marriage?'

'Maybe it was you,' she snapped back at him. 'You've changed, too. You didn't use to ask such obnoxious questions.'

He smiled slightly. 'You're almost not the same woman any more.'

'What did you expect?' she asked ironically, her brown eyes meeting his. 'Did you think I'd still be sobbing in that summer-house after six years?'

'I don't just mean that you've grown up. That's natural.' His sensual, authoritative mouth curved into that heart-melting smile. 'Or that you've grown from prettiness into beauty. That, too, was on the cards. I mean that you've become hard, bitter. That surprises me.'

'Does it really?' she rasped drily, unable to believe his lack of understanding. 'After what you did to me?'

'You've had six long years to get over that,' he reminded her. 'Are you saying you still haven't done so?'

'Of course not!'

'Just that you haven't forgiven me?'

Her smile was twisted. 'I wouldn't have thought forgiveness meant very much to a man in the pay of the devil. You've changed too, Damian. When I worked for you in Braythorpe, you were a high-flier with integrity. You had principles, and things mattered to you. Things other than success and money, I mean.'

'And now?' he asked gently.

'Now, from what I hear and read, you've become obsessed with success. At all costs.' She shortened her reins. 'It isn't just a case of a few dead fish, either, is it? People suffer, too. And when they want compensation, you're there to fob them off. The price of your success was turning your back on what you knew was right and just.'

The way his face had hardened told her that she'd struck home. 'I see you've been following my career,' he said in a flat voice.

'They have a way of making the news,' she shrugged. 'You've made quite a career out of exploiting people.'

He was sitting very still on his mount, his eyes darkening almost to black. 'That's not quite the way I would put it,' he said in a deceptively quiet voice.

'Oh?' She didn't bother to hide her scorn. 'And how *would* you put it?'

'It's unfortunate that the publicity machine loves clichés more than the truth.'

'A good answer,' she taunted. 'I remember a case, not so long ago, when a light aircraft belonging to a company you owned had crashed, and people had died. They claimed compensation. But you managed to keep the costs well down.' Her eyes glittered at him. 'At the expense of the victims' families.'

Now his eyes were as formidably cold as an arctic sea. 'You know nothing about that case, Kirby.'

'Tell me about it, then,' she invited drily.

'I never discuss my business affairs,' he said in a harsh voice.

'How convenient,' Kirby fluted, enjoying twisting the knife.

Wendy and Caroline were approaching now, and they could hear Wendy's clear, rather metallic voice saying, 'Daddy has an excellent relationship with darling Damian. After we get married, the two firms will probably merge into one really big company, with international affiliations. Daddy and darling Damian will be in charge, of course...'

'You're not being very fair, Kirby,' Damian said in a tight, low voice.

'Well, I'm not a very fair person, *darling Damian*,' she replied thinly, turning away. 'Anyway, why should you care? I'm nothing to you any more.'

'Whatever happens, you'll always be something to me, Kirby,' he said softly.

His words seemed to plunge a dagger into her vulnerable heart. 'Damn you, Damian,' she whispered bitterly. 'Don't treat me like—*oh*!'

Kirby broke off on a gasp. Her anger and nerves had somehow communicated themselves to her horse, which shied suddenly, snorting. Kirby wrestled for control as the animal wheeled. Her mount's rump slammed into the approaching Wendy. The blonde, lacking Kirby's instinctive control, was unable to keep herself in the saddle. She slid off her tottering horse, clutching vainly at the reins. There was a short scream and a muffled thump as she landed in the heather.

The three of them dismounted in concern. Wendy wasn't seriously hurt—the fragrant heather had cushioned her fall—but she was pale and angry, and liberally decorated with bits of leaf. She shook off Kirby's helping hand and apologetic words, her green eyes flashing.

'I'm all *right*,' she said tightly. 'It isn't the first time I've been knocked off a horse.' Damian's quiet amusement obviously wasn't helping her temper. 'Help me to remount, please, Damian,' she said shortly.

They passed through the gate, Damian and Wendy pairing up this time, leaving Kirby and Caroline to pick up the rear.

The exhilaration had quite gone from the afternoon. 'Damn,' Kirby muttered under her breath. 'I wish that hadn't happened. She looks as though she thinks it was my fault.'

'I should think she's fit to bust.' To her surprise, Kirby saw that Caroline was shaking with silent laughter. 'Can you blame her? First you go racing off with her fiancé, and then you knock her flying like some medieval knight at a joust. Good job she's well-built in the undercarriage department. Anyway,' Caroline pointed out, recovering herself, 'those beautiful fawn breeches needed breaking in. All right, Wendy?' she called aloud.

'Perfectly all right,' Wendy said, turning. But her eyes flashed a beam of pure dislike at Kirby.

And, though Caroline continued to snort with suppressed laughter for some time, Kirby couldn't find anything funny in the situation at all.

CHAPTER THREE

KIRBY eased the Jaguar through the gates of the Lodge, tyres crunching on gravel. The big, chocolate-brown limousine moved with luxurious smoothness and silence. With its power-assisted steering and automatic gearbox, it was certainly no effort to drive, not even for a woman as petite as Kirby Waterford.

But as she drove up the drive, she was thinking absently that she would definitely get rid of the car next week. She would ask Beeches Garage to sell it for her, and would arrange to buy something much smaller from them.

It was a relief to be getting back home. The impact of seeing Damian Holt again, after all these years, had shaken her. And being in such close proximity to him had been an ordeal she could have well done without, in her present fragile state. I'm not going to even think about him, she told herself firmly.

The crunching of gravel was muted by a carpet of autumn leaves as Kirby drove up to the house through the avenue of trees. Victorian red brick, the Lodge wasn't grand enough to justify its name. It wasn't even particularly beautiful, just a functional family home with a hard façade softened by streaks of ivy.

But the Lodge achieved stateliness by its position. Sited on a rise of land, backed by woods, it gazed magisterially down the valley towards the town of Braythorpe, North Yorkshire, where once upon a time the cotton magnate who had built this house could have contemplated the smoky mill town spinning prosperously six days a week, fifty-two weeks a year.

Now, a hundred and twenty years later, all but one of the mills had gone; and that one, tarted up with shutters and Virginia creeper, served as the Braythorpe Hotel. The hotel was usually full, even in autumn. Cotton was no longer king in Braythorpe, but other masters had come to the town, bringing employment to the townsfolk: iron and clay, glass and plastic, and, in this later age, the miniaturised components of all-powerful computers. The skilled workforce of this town had turned their hands and brains to whatever the tides of history and technology brought their way.

Getting out of the Jaguar in her mauve wool suit, Kirby turned automatically to look down at Braythorpe. A fine mist was descending from the hills, blurring the edges, softening the contours of the town hall, the two churches, the mill and the factories, the eternal cornerstones of Braythorpe. In this light, it looked almost pretty. Kirby smiled slightly, wondering whether anyone not brought up here could ever learn to love this sight.

Did Damian still feel his roots in this town? Did he still have any love for it left in his heart? She doubted that. He had shaken the provincial dust off his feet a long time ago, and the way his conversation showed an easy familiarity with cities such as New York, Milan, or Paris was an indication of just how far from his origins he had come.

Kirby turned and glanced at the other car parked in front of the Lodge. It was a dark red Rover, and her heart sank a little as she recognised it. It belonged to Roderick Braithwaite, the manager of Keith's factory—*her* factory, she corrected herself, getting her weekend bag out of the boot. Braithwaite was also one of the most powerful and troublesome members of the board of directors. She did not like the man. Wondering why he was here, Kirby locked the Jaguar, and walked up the stairs to the house.

Mrs Carstairs, her housekeeper, was waiting at the front door. She reached out to help Kirby with her bag.

'Mr Braithwaite's here, ma'am,' she said. 'He arrived about ten minutes ago, wanting to see you.'

'Did he say what it was in connection with?'

'No, ma'am.' Mrs Carstairs attended to the folds of her linen coat. 'I offered him a cup of tea, but he said he'd rather have a brandy.'

'Mr Braithwaite is a law unto himself, Mrs Carstairs,' Kirby replied, amused at the disapproval in the house-keeper's voice.

'Aye. He thinks he is, at any rate.'

Kirby checked herself in one of the big matching mirrors in the hall. 'If that offer of tea still stands, I'm a candidate. I'll just freshen myself up first. Tell Mr Braithwaite I won't keep him long.'

'Yes, ma'am.' The housekeeper folded Kirby's coat over her arm, and marched down the corridor.

Ten minutes later, refreshed and feeling better pre-pared to face Roderick Braithwaite, Kirby came down-stairs, and went straight to the yellow drawing-room. Her short, straight nose wrinkled quickly at the pungent smell of cigar-smoke that wreathed the air. And her feeling of distaste remained as she noted that Roderick was sitting in the high-backed leather armchair that had always been Keith's. Roderick was the only man she knew who would have sat in her dead husband's chair.

Roderick Braithwaite was conventionally handsome, yet there was something about him that always somehow reminded her of some predatory animal.

'Kirby,' he said, rising. 'You look ravishing. As ever.'

She submitted to Roderick's kiss, which was placed just off the corner of her mouth.

'Hello, Roderick. Nice to see you at the Lodge.'

Sharp teeth were showing in a smile. 'Well, if the mountain won't come to Mahomet, Mahomet must come to the mountain, eh? Invitations to the Lodge are all too few these days.' He waved the hand that held both the brandy glass and the cigar. 'Hope you don't mind, by the way?'

'Not at all.'

His eyes were travelling up and down her figure. 'That colour suits you, Kirby. You're a beautiful woman, and you look best in delicate colours. Mourning didn't become you. It was so Victorian. So...unfeminine. But let me get you a drink.'

'Mrs Carstairs will be bringing some tea for me in a short while. But you go ahead, by all means.' She moved to the mantelpiece, where a wood fire was waiting to be lit, and watched Roderick as he replenished his brandy glass.

He was, she knew, well over forty, a year or two older than Keith had been. A hard-headed Yorkshire businessman with ambition and drive. Not as clever as Keith, but far more ruthless.

'Good brandy, this,' Roderick commented. He strolled over to take a commanding place before the fire. 'Keith was a good judge of liquor.' His teeth glinted in a smile. 'And of other things. The old housekeeper tells me you spent the weekend at Caroline Langton's farm. You certainly move in the best circles these days.'

'Well, we're both widows, and we're close friends now. Did you want to speak to me about something in particular?'

'As it happens, I did.' He sat down again in Keith's chair, and crossed his legs. 'I'll get to the point. It's very simple. I've been offered the chairmanship of another company.'

Kirby raised slender eyebrows, genuinely surprised. 'Oh? Which company?'

'I'm afraid I'm not at liberty to say,' Roderick said smoothly. 'Shall we say that they're not so big nor so prestigious as Waterford Electronics, but that they have a great deal of potential. With the right leadership, they have a long, long way to go.' He paused with a fine sense of timing. 'They're in the same line of business as Waterford Electronics.'

'You're talking about Integrated Circuits,' Kirby said, so flatly that it was not a question.

'Now, now, I didn't say that.' His eyes gleamed as he enjoyed her evident discomposure. 'There are lots of new companies in our field, all trying to take our business away from us.'

'Whoever they are, you want to go over to the opposition.'

Mrs Carstairs opened the door to let a maid in with a tray of tea. The housekeeper froze momentarily as she caught sight of Roderick Braithwaite in the master's old chair, and her face tightened. She turned to Kirby.

'I'll light the fire, shall I, Mrs Waterford? That will clear the air.'

Kirby nodded, wondering how big a fire it would take to really clear the air between herself and Roderick Braithwaite.

There was no questioning the man's ability, of course. He had been Keith's virtual lieutenant for years. But there were many who'd questioned Keith's judgement when, as much out of recognition of Roderick Braithwaite's ambitious force of character as out of a desire to reward faithful service, he had allowed

Roderick to use an inheritance to buy enough voting stock to earn a seat on the board.

That had been about the time Keith and Kirby were getting married. Considering the strength of Roderick's character, and the way he'd managed to bully the weaker members since Keith Waterford's death, it was indeed hard to remember a time when Roderick Braithwaite had not been on the board.

She accepted a bone-china cup of fragrant tea from the maid. The fire started to crackle into yellow life, brightening the room.

When they were alone again, Kirby met Roderick's eyes. 'And are you going to accept this offer, Roderick?' she asked.

'Well, now. I can't deny that the offer has certain merits. I'm ready for a chairmanship. I know how to lead a business.' He gave her a brief, cunning glance. 'Of course, I'm very loyal to Waterford Electronics. I wouldn't give this offer a further thought if...well, if I had a clearer idea of my future at Waterford.'

'Your future at Waterford?' she repeated quietly.

'Aye. And the company's own future in the marketplace, come to that.'

'You sound as though you don't have confidence in the company's prospects.'

'Oh, I do. Up to a point. I've just had a look at the rough audit. Profits are going to be up again this quarter. That's thanks largely to me, I might add.'

Kirby laced her slim fingers, one elbow on the cool serpentine mantel. 'You and one or two others,' she said drily. 'You're an asset. But you don't run the show single-handed.'

'No. *You* do that, don't you?'

Colour rose to Kirby's high cheekbones at the deliberately pointed gibe. 'I'm not a financial genius,' she replied, fully aware of the implication of his words. 'I don't pretend to run Waterford Electronics. I just make sure that majority decisions of the board are passed without fuss. The board is doing an excellent job so far, and I have no complaints.'

'Aye. You're determined to keep Waterford Electronics squarely in the middle of the road, aren't you?' he said, with a dry note in his voice.

'Where else should it be?'

He rocked in front of the fire, exuding such a smug air of being in command, almost of being the owner here, that Kirby had to bite back her anger. 'Let me be blunt. Waterford Electronics needs someone at the helm, Kirby. There are big challenges ahead of us. We need to be able to make decisive responses and quick decisions. And we can't keep pouring our money away in benefits to the community. When the competition gets fiercer—and believe me, Kirby, it will get fiercer very soon—Waterford Electronics is going to need more than a caretaker. It's going to need a *leader*.'

'A leader like you.'

Roderick's face was flushed. 'You must realise that I can do the company, and you, a great deal of good as chairman. I want to pull Waterford Electronics out of the Dark Ages, Kirby. I can deliver bigger and faster profits than you've ever seen before! And I could really hurt you as chairman of a rival firm. After all,' he said sleekly, 'I'd not only be taking my experience and expertise with me. I'd also be taking a very intimate knowledge of Waterford Electronics's strong and weak points.'

Kirby watched him without responding. The flickering light from the fire was reflected in her pupils. The evening was growing cold and damp, and already the Lodge was shrouded in mist. Though normally she regarded fires as a waste, the ancient central heating of the Lodge was far from efficient, and tonight she was glad of the fire.

Had Roderick really been approached by a rival firm? Or had it been Roderick to approach them? Or was it all a bluff, designed to force her hand?

His mocking smile suggested that he knew exactly what sort of internal turmoil she was in.

'As a matter of interest,' she said mildly, 'just how would I stop Sir Malcolm Denison, and half the board with him, from resigning?'

Roderick's lips curled in contempt as he gulped down his brandy. 'Malcolm Denison can do as he pleases. I'm the only one capable of taking over from where Keith Waterford left off.'

'That's a big claim, Roderick,' Kirby said thinly. 'Sir Malcolm would certainly resign if I appointed you chairman over his head. And we can't afford to lose him. He's one of the finest business brains around.'

'Sir Malcolm's only concerned with lining his own nest. He hasn't the imagination to face the coming challenge. He's too old, Kirby.' Roderick's dark eyes locked with hers. 'His day is done. Let him resign, and good riddance. Waterford Electronics is changing direction.'

'Is it?'

'If you have the guts to recognise it, yes. Kirby, if you think you're rich now, I'll make you wealthy beyond your wildest dreams! I'll turn Waterford Electronics into the biggest money-spinner in the North! We'll get rid of all those grants and subsidies we currently make. They're nothing more than a waste of company profits. Just step down. Give me full power, as acting chairman, to take executive decisions. The company charter makes allowance for exactly that situation. I've checked it very thoroughly, I can assure you!'

'I'm sorry, Roderick,' she said.

'Are you refusing?'

'Yes.' She saw his eyes change to dark pools of anger. 'Keith left those shares to me because he thought I would look after the company he built from nothing—not so that I could hand it over to the first challenger who thought it was up for grabs.'

'Now listen, Kirby——'

'You've been an excellent chief manager, but you're not in line to be chairman of my husband's company. You must accept that, now and for ever.'

He was silent for a moment, breathing heavily through his nose, his lips tightly compressed. 'I admire you, Kirby. I really do. But you haven't heard my full offer yet.' He put his glass down on the mantel, and came towards her with an odd expression on his face. Kirby took an instinctive step backwards as he reached to grasp her arms. His fingers bit into her elbows, immobilising her. 'You've been a widow long enough, bonny lass. Half a year is plenty. It's time you thought about marrying again. Someone to take Keith's place. Someone strong and mature, someone who'll look after your interests in Waterford Electronics——'

'*You?*' she gasped, brown eyes widening in astonishment.

'Has it really never occurred to you before now?'

'Of course not, Roderick,' she said shakily.

His fingers tightened as his eyes burned into hers. 'I want you, Kirby. In my bed.'

She felt sick. 'You must be insane to even think——'

'I know you don't love me.' He grinned mirthlessly. 'But then, you didn't love Keith Waterford either, did you?'

'That's a despicable thing to say!' she gasped, paling.

'But a true one. You were too infatuated with that brilliant cousin of yours to love anyone but him.' She was struggling so fiercely that he was forced to let her go. 'Oh, I know I'm no Adonis, like Damian Holt. And I'm not a gentleman, like Keith was. But I'm man enough to run Waterford Electronics the way it should be run. And man enough to keep you satisfied in bed, I might add. Whatever the differences that led to my divorce with Susan, there was none of that sort of trouble. Now——'

'Don't say any more, please.' Her voice was trembling. She made an effort to restrain herself from showing her feelings of repulsion—she really did not want to hurt this man's feelings, whatever he was. 'Thank you for your proposal, unexpected as it was. But I'm not ready to re-marry, and I doubt whether I ever will be.' He made as if to argue, and she clenched her teeth. 'That's my last word, Roderick,' she said tightly.

'No, it's not,' he smiled smugly. 'Think about everything I've said, and consider the consequences. I think you'll find it an unmatchable offer. In the meantime, I think I'll take some leave I've got due.'

'Leave?' she echoed in confusion.

'I won't be in to the factory again, lass. Not unless it's as chairman.'

'You mean—you're tendering your resignation?'

'Let's just call it leave,' he grinned. 'For the time being, anyway.'

'You can't do that,' Kirby said quietly. 'Your contract binds you to giving at least six weeks' notice of resignation.'

'What are you going to do?' He looked amused. 'Slap my wrist?'

Kirby followed him to the door on shaky legs, feeling a sense of impending dread in her heart.

Roderick swung back on her at the front door. 'Sleep on it, Kirby. You'll see how right I am.' He kissed her cheek, and Kirby watched him get into his Rover.

When the tail-lights were out of sight in the heavy mist, Kirby went back into the house, and picked up the telephone to call Sir Malcolm Denison.

There had been fifteen years between Kirby's late husband and Sir Malcolm, an age difference which hadn't interfered with their close friendship. At fifty-seven, Sir Malcolm Denison was beginning to take on the distinguished air of an elder statesman. Knighted a few years ago for his work with an ailing wing of a now de-nationalised industry, he wore his title and his years with a pompous manner which rather suited him.

He had his finger in a great many pies these days, though few as profitable as the WEC pie. He was the second largest shareholder in Waterford Electronics, after Kirby herself. Roderick was the third largest.

Between the three of them they dominated the board. But Kirby's position was anomalous. She didn't have enough shares on her own to impose her will on the firm without serious problems. She could only do that with support from either one of the other two—and preferably with the support of both.

So far, the alliance had held, though she'd been aware of its increasing fragility.

And though her husband had liked both men, for different reasons, he had fully trusted neither. And it was the memory of Keith's distrust, more than any other factor, that had stopped Kirby from letting either man grasp at the chairmanship, even though she would have liked nothing better than to resign, and let someone else take on the responsibility.

She told Malcolm what had happened with Roderick Braithwaite. She didn't tell Malcolm about Roderick's crude proposal of marriage. But she passed on his ultimatum about resigning.

'He's going to be a great loss to Waterford Electronics,' Sir Malcolm sighed portentously. 'This is a serious blow. Braithwaite was a bully-boy, but definitely a great asset to the company. I don't know how we'll replace him. This has been a bad miscalculation, Kirby.'

She stiffened. 'I'm not sure I understand the word "miscalculation".'

'Perhaps I should have said a set-back. Quite apart from anything else, Braithwaite is going to hand the opposition a disastrous amount of insider knowledge about Waterford Electronics and its doings. A great pity. Perhaps if the situation had been handled differently...'

'Differently? He gave me an ultimatum, Malcolm. The chairmanship, on a plate, or he would resign.'

'Of course, I'm not criticising you in the slightest. I'm sure you did the best you could. But possibly if Braithwaite had been dealing with someone a little more experienced, this dilemma might have been avoided...'

Kirby smiled tightly without interrupting as Sir Malcolm went on. She'd anticipated that, with Roderick gone, Sir Malcolm would start his own bid for the chairmanship by and by, but she hadn't expected him to get his attack into gear quite so quickly!

'Controlling men like Braithwaite takes a firm hand,' he was saying. 'Come to that, controlling most men in business takes a firm hand. One needs a great deal of character, experience and tact. It takes considerable skills, really, to make a good chairman.'

'Yes. So Roderick Braithwaite was telling me,' Kirby said calmly.

Sir Malcolm cleared his throat. 'Of course, the idea of a man like Braithwaite chairing the board at Waterford Electronics is preposterous.'

'Exactly what I told him.'

'But, in general terms, a strong leadership would be the best thing for the company. We need to make changes, substantial changes, to the way things are run.'

'Do we?'

'Yes. We could make Waterford Electronics a great deal more profitable than it is, Kirby. Of course, I mean that with no disrespect to Keith's memory. In fact, the person who chairs the board needs to be someone who was close to Keith Waterford. Someone who understood his ideals. Someone who has the best interests of the company, and indeed the whole Waterford family, at heart.'

'Quite. Which was why,' she said succinctly, 'Keith left the biggest share of the stock to me.'

Sir Malcolm was evidently taken aback. 'Well, that of course was Keith's intention for the interim. Until a more—ah, permanent solution could be found.'

'I have no intention of standing down in the immediate future.'

'Not for Braithwaite, you mean.'

'Not for anyone,' she said firmly.

'I'm sure you'll want to reconsider that stance soon, Kirby. After all, you must want to get back to your own life. To have wealth without having to administer it is a very rare privilege. You don't want to spend the next twenty years worrying about Waterford Electronics, do you?'

Kirby's heart sank heavily. Sir Malcolm, too, was manoeuvring her into a corner.

'Well,' he said, 'we'll need to discuss this at a full board meeting, very soon. Shall I call one for Friday next week?'

'Yes,' Kirby said heavily, 'I suppose you'd better.'

'We're going to miss Braithwaite,' he told her heavily. 'Miss him badly.'

Ironically, Kirby noted the fake regret in Sir Malcolm's voice. No doubt Sir Malcolm was feeling intense delight that his biggest rival within Waterford Electronics was apparently going, that no direct blame for Roderick's resignation could attach to the name of Sir Malcolm Denison, and that he himself had not had to deal with Roderick.

'Hypocrite' was the word that rose in Kirby's mind.

Far from backing her up, or showing any gratification that Kirby had defended his position against Roderick Braithwaite, Malcolm, she knew, was going to use this incident against her. Possibly even to further attack her standing with the remainder of the board.

But that, she knew by now, was the nature of the game.

It was so difficult, there was so much she did not understand, and felt she would never understand. The past ten months had been a terrible strain for her. Damian had called it a crushing burden, and, as usual, his choice of words had been deadly accurate.

Just getting a grasp of how Waterford Electronics was run, and understanding the implications of the decisions that constantly had to be taken, had been crushing.

And now this. She was under no illusions about Sir Malcolm Denison. Not any more. Friday after next was going to be a watershed, a meeting at which Malcolm was going to press hard, very hard, to be given the chairmanship. Her standing with the rest of the board was going to be very shaky in the wake of Roderick Braithwaite's resignation, and she was going to find it very hard to fight off a concerted attack.

She had until Friday after next to find a way of doing so.

* * *

Later, as she ate sparingly in the kitchen, alone as always, there was a tap at the door, and she turned tiredly to face Mrs Carstairs. 'A call for you, Mrs Waterford.'

'Who is it from?'

'Mr Damian Holt, ma'am.' She saw Kirby put down her knife and fork and close her eyes in misery, and added sympathetically, 'Shall I tell him you'll call back?'

'No,' Kirby said with an effort, 'I'll speak to him.' She went into the drawing-room and picked up the telephone, her throat tight. 'Kirby Waterford speaking.'

'Hello, Kirby,' came the deep-timbred tones down the line. 'Everything all right?'

'Of course,' she said in a brittle voice. 'Why?'

'You sounded a bit rattled,' Damian commented.

'I'm perfectly all right. What is this call about, Damian?'

'I'm having lunch at L'Escargot tomorrow. Would you like to join me? We haven't really had a chance to talk about old times yet.'

It was typical of him to choose the most expensive restaurant in the area, but there was an underlying significance to L'Escargot, in that it had been the place he'd used to take her, in the old days, when they'd had something really special to celebrate. The very name brought back tingling memories.

'I doubt whether Wendy would be very interested in our old times, Damian,' she replied stiffly.

'Wendy won't be coming. She went back to London this morning, for a week.'

'I see. While the cat's away...is that it?'

He laughed softly. 'Exactly. See you tomorrow, then?'

Her anger flared up.

'No, Damian,' she said sharply, 'I do not want to have lunch with you tomorrow. Not even if you *have* just sent your fiancée back to her daddy in London. In case you haven't got the message, I don't want to see you again—anywhere or any time!'

'Kirby——'

'Whatever we had to say to each other,' she went on passionately, cutting him off, 'was all said six years ago. Kindly remember that.'

She was shaking with emotion, but when Damian's voice came back on the line, it was as calm as though her outburst just hadn't happened. 'I'll be there at one-thirty. Come if you change your mind.'

The line clicked dead in her ear.

Damn him to hell. She felt like bursting into tears, but now was not the time to give in to foolish feminine weakness. She took another couple of deep breaths to steady herself, then walked to the window, and stared out into the night. In her mind she was hearing again those softly spoken words on the hillside. Whatever happens, you'll always be something to me.

Now was the time to turn to him for help. He had offered, hadn't he? Why let stupid pride stop her from accepting?

Because of the way he hurt me, something inside her replied. Humiliated me. Scarred me.

Her eyes lost their focus. Her eighteenth birthday. The day Damian had chosen to let her know how things really stood between them.

There had been a party. It was not a happy occasion. It had been one fraught with pain and tension because of what had been happening between her and Damian lately. Over the past few months, Kirby had been making her feelings about him abundantly clear. She loved Damian with every fibre of her being, and she had not tried to hide her adoration from him.

Yet it was as though the more she showed him her love, the more he replied with cruelty and indifference.

As though he was deliberately trying to wound her in the most agonisingly sensitive area of her feelings. He rebuffed her constantly, and not just when they were alone; at the office, in front of others, he had delivered stinging snubs that had left her with swimming eyes and a bleeding heart.

In fact, coming to work was starting to turn into a daily ordeal that she dreaded. Nothing she did seemed to please or satisfy him any more. Her best efforts met with cold indifference, while the smallest error earned her swift, harsh, incisive criticism.

What was almost worse, he was seeing other women constantly, a lot of other women, and taking care that she saw it, or heard about it. It was as though he took pleasure in flaunting his sexual prowess in front of Kirby, showing her how many women could be got to throw themselves at his feet.

It didn't make her love him less. It just hurt her more and more, and sank her deeper into bewilderment.

She soon learned that there was one simple solution—and that was to stay well away from him. But, easy as that sounded, she couldn't do it. She loved him, and there was nothing she could do but be drawn to him, sucked into the dark maelstrom of his fatal attraction for her.

She was aware of the spectacle she was starting to make, aware of the sniggers, the pity, the staring eyes. But she could no more have helped herself than someone caught in a whirlpool.

Those who cared about her had tried to warn her. Even her mother, concerned and anxious, had tried to remonstrate, tell her that she was heading for heartbreak. But it had done no good. She'd been lost, still swirling helplessly around the elemental force that was Damian Holt.

She hadn't understood. Why was he doing this to her? They'd been so close all their lives, more like two sides of one soul than like separate people. She'd always loved him. Why now, now that she was old enough to give that love a physical expression, had he turned against her?

She knew she was pretty, that her slim figure drew the attention of most men. Other men desired her, and, if she'd wanted to, she could have had almost as many conquests as Damian. Yet when she was with him he made her feel so unattractive, so uninteresting. And the prettier she made herself, the worse he treated her.

Her eighteenth birthday, theoretically bringing full adulthood, had been coming up fast. But understanding was a long, long way behind. And, at the party, he had chosen to break her heart, once and for all time.

Her eyes were drawn up to the portrait of Keith's gentle, serious face which always hung over the desk which had once been his, and which she now used for her correspondence.

You didn't love Keith Waterford.

Braithwaite's cruel words had been untrue. She had loved the man who had been her husband for five happy years, but it had been a very different kind of love. There had always been something missing for her. No matter whom she'd married, there would always have been something missing.

She could only pray that Keith had never sensed that gap in their relationship. She felt sure he had not. Deep passion and deep pain had not been a part of Keith Waterford's nature.

He had never thrilled her the way Damian had done. But then, he had never wounded her in the same dreadful way, either.

Keith had given her back her sanity and her self-respect. And she would always owe him that. Kirby closed her eyes. Which was why she knew she was going to meet Damian at L'Escargot for lunch. She owed it to Keith Waterford to preserve the company he'd put so much of himself into. And, right now, Damian Holt was the one man who might be able to help her do that.

CHAPTER FOUR

IT WAS years since Kirby had last been to L'Escargot, but the restaurant had changed little since then, and the French head waiter recognised her immediately. He seemed genuinely touched to see her again, and pressed her hand to his lips gallantly before leading her to the alcove seat looking out over the garden, where Damian was already waiting, a dark and dazzlingly handsome figure.

He rose to greet her, looking unsurprised that she had turned up despite her refusal of last night. Kirby was overcome by a choking moment of nostalgia as she allowed Damian to kiss her cool cheek, but she fought the weakness down.

'As you can see,' she said neutrally, 'I changed my mind.'

'I thought you might.'

Kirby gave him a dry look to punish his vanity. She unslung her practical leather shoulder-bag, and put it under the table as she sat down. She was wearing a lavender tweed suit this morning, with a silk blouse and pearls. One of her most formal, and most expensive, outfits. The beauty it conferred on her was remote, cold, very different from her usual warm earthiness.

For his part, Damian was wearing a charcoal alpaca suit that set off his dark, rich colouring to perfection. Against the deep gold of his skin, his dark blue eyes were startling, and the silver wings in the black hair added a devastating touch of distinction. The deep, curving laughter-lines on either side of his mouth were

57

emphasised, as though he was secretly entertained by her arrival. The crow's-feet at his eyes were also suspiciously amused.

He looked painfully desirable, and Kirby felt again, with an aching heart, that no man would ever affect her the way Damian did.

They were undeniably a handsome couple, and her entrance had caused a slight stir in the muted hubbub of conversation. People were still looking at them, and she knew that a lot of the diners here knew who they were. By next week, she thought wryly, tongues would be wagging all over Yorkshire.

Damian was watching her. 'You're beautiful,' he said quietly, eyes seeming to flame at her from under the dark brows.

'Oh, please,' she retorted with brittle irritation, 'let's not play the fool, Damian. I haven't come here to flirt with you, or play games of let's remember.'

'No?' The magnificent golden face was amused. 'What have you come for, then?'

'On business,' she said brusquely.

'Business?' She saw his eyes drop to her breasts. With dismay she realised that reaction had hardened her nipples flagrantly against the fine silk blouse, making two peaks that, to another man, might have been an erotic invitation. Flushing, she pulled her jacket over herself.

'Considering what happened between us six years ago, and considering that you are now engaged to Wendy Catchpole,' she said icily, 'bandying compliments with me is in especially poor taste.'

'What business are you here on, then?' he enquired, arching one dark eyebrow.

'You offered your advice the other day,' she reminded him, still without warmth. 'Does that offer still stand?'

He shrugged his broad shoulders slightly. 'Yes, of course. But whatever you came for, I'm glad to see you. Can we order lunch before we get down to it?'

'Whatever you like.' She accepted the menu he passed her, and took less than thirty seconds to pick a salad, a steak, and a fresh fruit salad to follow.

While Damian discussed the question of wines with the *sommelier*, she stared out of the window at the garden, which was carpeted with gold and crimson leaves from the big beeches that screened the restaurant from the road. The very atmosphere of this place was a pain in the heart for her. It reminded her so much of the helpless love she'd once felt for Damian.

She emerged from her reverie to find Damian watching her intently, lids hooding those slaty eyes.

'What are you thinking?' she asked him shortly.

'Things I've been forbidden to say,' he replied with a slight smile. 'I might ask you the same question.'

'I was thinking about those trees. They're bigger than they were last time we ate here together.'

'Time passes quickly these days. When we were kids, a year was forever. Now the years come and go so fast that we hardly notice them flying. Where did the years go, Kirby?'

There was a perilous lump in her throat. 'I don't know. I'd prefer to talk about my problem with Waterford Electronics, if you don't mind.'

'Does it upset you to be here, with me?' He reached across the table, lean fingers closing around hers. She jumped at the warm possession of his hands, and forced herself not to pull away, and show him just how much he affected her.

'It brings back memories, but it doesn't upset me,' she said stiffly.

'Good,' he purred. He was stroking the backs of her hands with his thumbs, an achingly sensual caress. 'I'm glad you came to me with your problems, Kirby. I'm glad you felt you could trust me.'

I don't trust you, she almost snapped. Could he tell that her palms were suddenly damp with perspiration, her pulses racing at his touch? She gulped with relief as he released her, and turned thankfully to her salad when it arrived.

'Go ahead,' Damian invited, 'I'm listening.'

Over the sophisticated salad of shrimps, scallops and other seafood, she tried to give him some of the background to what had started happening this week. Though she'd meant to keep it concise, she found herself talking at some length, one subject leading into the next until she had covered the ground thoroughly.

Damian listened carefully as she talked.

'Did Keith leave you his total holding of stock?' he asked.

'Yes,' she nodded.

'You're the actual owner, not a trustee?' She nodded again to confirm that. 'As I said the other night, that makes you a very rich woman, Kirby.'

'As I said the other night—only on paper,' she replied tersely. 'I'm not interested in money, Damian. Only in doing what's right for the company.'

He considered her thoughtfully. When Damian concentrated, that ruthlessly handsome face took on a slightly sombre look. You realised that it was the glittering eyes, the expressions, that made him seem so affable. Beneath that debonair mask, she knew, lay deeper and more powerful depths. Whirlpool depths. That broad forehead and those aristocratically carved temples framed a mind that was razor-sharp, humming with power.

She finished off by explaining in full what had happened between her and Roderick on Monday, and Sir Malcolm Denison's reaction on the telephone.

'And now Malcolm has obviously seen his chance, with Roderick out of the way. He's already started piling on the pressure. Insinuating that I'm incompetent, wanting to take over. There's a board meeting Friday next week, and I just know that he's going to make a concerted attack on me.'

'I thought Sir Malcolm Denison was Keith's best friend?'

'Keith liked Roderick, too, but he didn't trust him further than he could see him. It's just business.' Kirby closed her eyes tiredly for a moment. 'While the two of them were clashing heads, things were more or less evened up. If Roderick goes—and, incidentally, he hasn't turned up at the factory today—Malcolm will have the field to himself. I'm so tired of it all, Damian. I just don't know what to do any more...'

'The man who says he's resigning—Roderick Braithwaite. What's he like?'

Kirby lifted her hands. 'Big. Brash. Middle-aged. A pusher and shover, with more ambition than finesse. But with enough energy to push and shove his way to the chairmanship.'

'He hasn't actually handed in his notice yet?'

'No.'

Damian was watching her over his steepled fingers. 'Anything else about him I should know?'

Kirby hesitated, feeling her face flush hotly. 'Well, he thought I might as well marry him while I was about it.'

Damian's eyes glittered darkly. 'He proposed marriage?'

She nodded. 'Yes.'

'And?'

'And nothing,' she shrugged.

'You aren't interested?' Damian said sharply.

'I didn't say that,' Kirby replied steadily. 'I haven't given him an answer either way. Not yet.'

Damian's eyes didn't leave hers. 'But you can't seriously be considering this man's proposal?'

'Why not?' Kirby asked back.

'You've just described him as brash, aggressive, and middle-aged. Not exactly your type.'

'As Caroline said the other night, this is a hard world for a woman on her own.' She was starting to rather enjoy that angry glitter in his eyes. 'Having a brash husband might have its attractions. As for his being middle-aged...' Kirby dissected her steak calmly '...he's really quite handsome, in his way. And, let's face it, I wouldn't be marrying for love. Not again.'

Damian growled. 'You've just said yourself that he simply wants Waterford Electronics, on a plate.'

'I also said that he has plenty of energy. With someone behind him to direct that energy, who knows?' She glanced at Damian coolly. 'It might be a solution. I certainly haven't discounted it.'

Damian was obviously making an effort to keep his poise. 'But if wedding-bells don't chime, he says he's going to accept a chairmanship with one of Waterford Electronics's competitors—taking his knowledge of the company with him?'

Kirby nodded.

'And Sir Malcolm Denison?' he asked. 'Why don't you trust him to run Waterford Electronics?'

'For the same reason that I don't trust Roderick Braithwaite. Because he likes money too much.'

'Isn't business all about money?' Damian enquired, arching one eyebrow slightly.

'No, Damian. You know that as well as I do.' She had no appetite to finish her steak, delicious as it was. She pushed her plate away, and leaned back in the leather chair, curly chestnut hair framing a face that was slightly pale with weariness and strain. 'Banking might be all about money, but running a company like Waterford Electronics isn't. Money is a by-product, perhaps the most important by-product, but it isn't the sole objective.'

Damian's eyes drifted over the slight, feminine figure across the table from him. 'That's only one way of looking at it.'

'But it's *my* way,' she retorted emphatically. 'We both know that there are many methods of running a big company. There's a balanced middle way, and there are extremes on either side. Someone like Sir Malcolm Denison would run Waterford Electronics to make himself rich. To make as much money in as short a period as possible. Just as one example, Waterford Electronics has always made a lot of charitable contributions in Braythorpe. Scholarships, grants, subsidies to sports centres. We've sponsored a charity marathon. Currently, we're helping set up a retraining scheme. That kind of thing. It comes out of profits, and it's expensive, but I want that to continue, just as it's always done. Malcolm keeps pressuring me to stop all that.'

'Surely you can compromise on such a minor issue?'

'That's just the tip of the iceberg. There are bigger and more serious problems beneath.'

'Such as?'

She sighed. 'The firm has massive assets. Subsidiaries, investments, plant, land, buildings. Chopped up into pieces and sold off, that could all create a lot of fast liquid capital.'

'And make you an even richer woman than you are now,' he pointed out calmly.

She drained her glass, watched by those dark blue eyes. 'Yes. There'd be a mountain of money. But Waterford Electronics would have changed completely. It would no longer be a caring company, with responsibilities, with a tradition of helping the town. Braythorpe would have lost something for ever. I may not know much about business, but I know enough to stop that from happening.'

Damian was resting his chin on his fist, dark eyes hooded, his passionate mouth brooding. 'Is this Keith speaking?'

She met his eyes. 'It's Kirby.'

The waiter materialised beside them, and they sat in silence as he cleared the table, and brought Kirby her fruit salad, and Damian his glass of brandy.

Kirby hesitated, stirring the pudding with her spoon. 'Damian...what can I do?'

He laced long tanned fingers around his brandy glass. 'I'll have to consider it. There are various solutions to this kind of situation, and it's a case of coming up with the best one available.' He inhaled the bouquet of the cognac, then tasted it. 'We'll have to do a lot of talking, of course. See a fair bit of one another. You gave me the impression that you might find that...difficult.'

She stared at him. Her heart was thudding again, a fist pounding mercilessly against her. Damian. Damian was offering to come back into her life again. If she said *yes* now, she would see him again. And after that, and after that. Until he went back to London, and left her craving him, the way an addict craved a drug. He was fatal to her, her nemesis.

But, in her present wilderness, who else could help her? She had no one to turn to any more.

'I need your help.' Her own voice sounded dry and harsh in her ears. She'd been almost unaware of forming the words.

Damian inclined his dark head. 'Then I'll give it.'

'Thank you,' she all but whispered. She was suddenly tired, so very tired. She could almost have burst into tears with sheer emotion.

Damian had taken out a crocodile-skin notepad, and was writing in it with a heavy gold pen. She watched the slick nib move across the paper. 'I'll get in touch with Braithwaite and Denison this afternoon, if you'll give me their numbers. I have a feeling that's where I should begin. I'll also want to talk to whoever is your company lawyer, and, if possible, the accountant.'

'You'll be discreet?' she begged.

'No, I'll go in like the commandos,' he said ironically. 'First I'll kick the door down, then I'll spray them with machine-gun fire. What do you think I am, Kirby?'

'Sorry.' She pulled open her bag, and took out her own diary to give him the basic information he wanted.

'We won't discuss this any further right now,' he decided. 'You look exhausted. I'll call and see you at the Lodge this evening. OK?'

Kirby nodded, and pushed her bowl away, leaving the fruit salad, too, almost untasted. Damian met her eyes. 'You've had a tough time of it, haven't you?' he asked quietly.

'I'm not as frail as I look,' she said.

'Yes,' Damian observed with a dry look on his tanned face. 'I learned that, Kirby. Long ago.' He drained the rest of his brandy, and smiled at her. 'You talk about Braythorpe with quite a proprietorial air,' he said lazily. 'Is the town really that important to you?'

'Yes,' she said with a flash of anger. 'I haven't sold *my* soul for a fat London bank account, Damian. Not yet. This town meant something to Keith. And to me. I was born here. So were Mum and Dad, and their parents before them.'

'And so was I,' Damian said mildly.

'You wouldn't think so,' she snapped. 'Nothing here seems to matter a damn to you, *darling Damian*. Does anything matter to you in London?'

He didn't answer, just kept watching her with those dark, brilliant eyes. Kirby rubbed her temples, her anger fading. 'I'm sorry. I'm tired, and I shouldn't have snapped.'

'I wanted to see whether you would snap,' Damian said with a slight smile. 'At least I know where you stand.'

'I'm not a businesswoman, Damian. Unlike you, I can't reconcile myself to exploiting human misery.'

His eyes darkened angrily. 'Is that what I do?'

'It's what you did to those Third World fishermen! It's what you did to the family of that boy who was killed in that plane crash!'

He seemed to be making an effort to bite back a reply. 'I told you, I don't discuss my business affairs,' he said at last. 'But let me put it hypothetically. Accidents happen. People get hurt at work. That's human nature. Big companies often get the blame, even when negligence can be proven against the victims. We don't like to see people suffer. We try to pay out what we're liable for. But it doesn't always work that way.'

'No?' she asked aloofly.

'No.' Damian held her gaze. 'Sometimes some hotshot lawyer rushes round to see the family in his Ferrari, and starts convincing them that he can make their fortunes by suing the company on their behalf. It doesn't matter whether the company was at fault or not. They have all the money, don't they? Long before a compensation figure has even been calculated, he's already started talking in terms of millions.' His fingers were drumming a devil's tattoo on the table, an old sign of impatience. 'In the meantime experts start working out a realistic figure. When it's announced, it's way below the figure the hot-shot lawyer has come to. The hot-shot lawyer advises the families, now his clients, to reject the offer. He holds a Press conference to create a blaze of publicity, which ends up focused on him. Then, with the sword of justice in his good right hand, he leads a crusade against the company.'

'Please. Spare me the cynicism.'

Damian smiled without humour. 'Right. The company has to defend the case. It's no longer a question of the company and the families any more. Now it's their lawyers against our lawyers. The case drags on for months. All this time, the victims' families still haven't received any compensation. Legal fees mount up to immense figures on both sides. When a settlement is finally reached, after agonising and embittering delays, the hot-shot lawyer scoops a massive dollop off the top. The families end up with less than they'd have got if they hadn't contested, all those months ago. The hot-shot lawyer, after making a pious statement to the Press, drives back to his penthouse in his Ferrari, with a large cheque in his pocket. And the families wonder what it was all about, anyway.' Damian leaned forward grimly. 'Now you tell me. Which one of us is profiting off human misery? The company or the hot-shot lawyer? Which of us has perverted the course of justice?'

'You're talking about a hypothetical case,' Kirby replied, not wanting to show how much his rhetoric had swayed her. 'Are you saying that's what happened with the plane crash?'

'I'm saying that I don't specialise in defrauding widows and orphans, Kirby. The tabloid Press are not qualified as moral commentators. If you want the truth, check the court records yourself.'

He was really angry, Kirby realised. Her knife had somehow slid through a chink in that massive armour of his, and had touched a vital spot. Knowing that she had hurt him gave her an odd feeling, part-triumph, part-pain.

'Well,' she said with well-feigned lightness, reaching for her bag, 'I'm not too proud to call on your services. So why should I worry about muddying my skirts? I'd like to pay for this meal, Damian.'

'You can't,' he said calmly. 'I invited you.'

She checked her watch artlessly. 'Is that the time? I'm so sorry, I have to run. I have an appointment at three.'

He rose, his eyes glinting, but kept his urbane mask in place. 'I'll see you tonight.'

'Good.' She was backing away, keeping herself out of reach of any possible goodbye kisses. 'I look forward to that. Thank you for helping, Damian. I appreciate it.'

She gave him a bright smile, and turned to leave.

She felt his dark eyes boring into her back all the way out of the restaurant.

CHAPTER FIVE

KIRBY got home at five, and changed out of her lavender tweed into her more usual home attire—denim jeans and a cotton shirt, with a fluffy white angora sweater to keep her warm. It was more 'her' than the elegant, formal clothes she was forced to wear as head of Waterford Electronics, and Keith Waterford's widow.

Damian hadn't said what time he would call, and she distracted herself by pottering around the house, doing all the household tasks she'd been putting off.

The Lodge was so big without Keith. Its emptiness echoed around her mournfully, the stately rooms filled with an air of melancholy which was emphasised by the covers she'd had put on the furniture in the rooms that were no longer used.

She would have sold the Lodge, as she was currently selling the Jaguar, if she'd been able to do so. But the house was tied up with the assets of Waterford Electronics. Nor was there any way she could have dismissed Mrs Carstairs, who'd been housekeeper here for years. In fact, she welcomed Mrs Carstairs's company in the big house; they were not intimate, but they had become friends.

When darkness fell, and an evening mist started to form round the house, Mrs Carstairs had the maid prepare a fire in the drawing-room. Feeling wearied, Kirby made herself a mug of coffee, and sat beside the fire, staring with unseeing eyes at the flames that flickered around the logs.

Damian would be here soon. Despite the fire, and the downy luxury of her angora jersey, she felt a cold chill touch her skin.

Her thoughts had gone back six years in time, to that fateful night of her eighteenth birthday.

She'd been so young, then. So young, and so vulnerable. Eighteen had been the gateway to adulthood—so they told her—but she'd felt so very helpless.

At least Damian hadn't done what Kirby had dreaded he might do, which was bring another girl to her party, dance with her, flirt with her, and take her home, leaving Kirby in floods of tears. In fact, it had been a pleasant enough, ordinary party. Ordinary, that was, until the end.

Because after the party, lovesick and hopelessly infatuated with Damian, she'd thought a miracle had happened.

Everyone had gone home, or gone to bed, except the two of them. She had found herself alone with Damian, in the dark garden, on the cold, crystal-clear December night of her eighteenth year.

She'd wanted to thank him for his kindness, and she'd started saying so; but somehow tears had got in the way, choking her words and bringing her to a halt.

And then she'd been in Damian's arms, hearing the half-stifled groan, deep in his chest, as his lips had sought hers. It had been a kiss like nothing else she'd ever experienced, or was to experience again. His mouth had seemed to sear hers, his arms crushing her with such formidable strength that she was dizzy.

She'd heard him whisper the words she thought she would never hear from him.

'Kirby... my darling... I want you so much.'

A miracle. Kirby's soul had soared, leaving her body, reaching heights of bliss that she'd never dreamed of. It was as though all the months of pain and tension had been swept away. All her misery was over. He loved her. He felt exactly the way she did; she could tell that by the way his strong arms trembled, by the way his voice caught in his throat as he whispered her name.

As she strained against him, their tongues meeting in the flickering excitement of their first real kiss, she'd had the wild thought that the past months of misery had been some kind of test, some kind of ordeal that he'd put her through to find out whether her feelings would survive.

They'd slipped into the summer-house at the bottom of the garden, which offered shelter from the December cold, and he'd taken her in his arms again. His hunger had been almost pagan, his mouth devouring her lips, her throat, the upraised oval of her face. His arousal had been hot and thrusting against her. She felt his hands caress her taut breasts, brushing the aching peaks of her nipples in a release that had made her gasp huskily with pleasure.

They knew each other so well, bodies and minds; they had seen one another grow from adolescence into maturity. But it had never been like this before. This was a fulfilment of the promise that had built up over all those years, like the vast weight of water behind a dam, waiting for the floodgates to open and release that long-pent-up pressure.

Kirby moved away from the window, and walked back across the room, feeling her face flushing hotly with the six-year-old memories. Even now, at this great distance of time and experience, her pulses were racing at the recollection of what she'd felt that night. Pleasures and pains that nothing, nothing at all, had ever come close to since then.

That night in the summer-house had ended in near hysteria for Kirby. The ecstasy of their embrace had been ruptured savagely, without warning. She'd felt the reaction rip through Damian's big body, muscles bunching as he'd tensed, then had thrust her harshly away from him.

'For God's sake,' he'd snarled in a voice like a stranger's, 'what are you doing to me?'

She'd covered her aroused, tingling breasts, and had stared him numbly in the darkness. 'Damian, I love you,' she'd whispered in bewilderment.

'Love?' he'd ground out. 'You don't know what you're talking about.'

'I do,' she'd pleaded, trying to take him in her arms again, 'I do! We're meant for each other; you know that.'

'What are you talking about?' he'd asked dangerously.

'About you and me. I always thought you knew how I felt. That I want to be your wife. That we'd—we'd— get married one day——'

'Married?' That was when he'd really erupted. He'd thrust her away with such violence that she'd staggered, gasping with the pain that had been neither physical nor mental, but something crueller, more frightening. Kirby had quailed, terrified and uncomprehending under the savage words that followed.

'I've known you since you were a child, but I never realised you were such a fool.'

'Wh-what do you mean?' she'd whispered, appalled.

'Haven't you got the message by now? I don't want you around me any more. I've outgrown you! I've been trying to tell you that for months, and you're just too damned bone-headed to understand.'

'Damian!'

'Did you think otherwise?' he'd challenged fiercely, a dark silhouette against the window.

'I thought you cared!'

'What gave you that impression?' he'd asked contemptuously.

'You—you've always cared! Why did you give me that job in your firm, if you didn't want me near you?'

'Just to help out. As a stepping-stone so that you could move on to something more permanent. I didn't expect that you'd outstay your welcome so long, mooning over me like a lovesick girl.'

She'd buried her face in her hands, sobbing at the cruelty, the unjustness of it. He'd been pitiless as he went on.

'As for marriage, you can get *that* idea out of your head right away. For one thing, I have no room in my life for a wife, and, for another, I wouldn't choose you, anyway.' His voice had grown quieter, but not any more gentle. 'You might as well know, here and now, that I'm leaving Braythorpe.'

That had shocked her out of her tears. 'Leaving?' she'd gasped.

'I'm going to London. Soon. That's where my career lies, and I don't think I'll ever be coming back.' He'd stepped forward, and had grasped her shoulders, fingers biting into her flesh. 'Listen to me, Kirby. There's nothing between us. We were good friends; we could still have been good friends. But you chose to confuse friendship with love, and that has spoiled everything. The best advice I can give you now is to forget all about me, and forget all about love, until you meet someone who's prepared to return your feelings.'

He'd turned and walked out, leaving her in hysterical tears, beyond hope.

There was a tap at the door, mercifully interrupting her thoughts.

Kirby dragged herself out of the dark well of her memories, and turned to face Mrs Carstairs. 'Yes, Mrs Carstairs?'

'I'm just knocking off, Mrs Waterford. There's a cottage pie in the fridge. Is there anything else before I leave?'

'No, thank you,' she said automatically. 'You're very kind to me, Mrs Carstairs. See you tomorrow.'

She leaned back in the leather chair, one hand against her aching heart. Remembering that dreadful night had brought it all back. The near-breakdown that had followed, the black, empty winter that had enveloped her.

God, what an empty, bottomless abyss she'd fallen into.

She'd left work, of course. And Damian, as he'd promised, had gone to London, his career soaring above the mundane heights of other men. Her loneliness and grief had been intense, endless.

It had been Keith who had rescued her, in the summer of the following year. Gentle, kind Keith who had cared for her so much, who hadn't minded that her heart was somewhere else. He had loved her for what she was, not for what she could give him, or do for him. Older than her, older even than Damian, he had already been a wealthy man, his computer electronics company enjoying a big, solid success. He had drawn her out of the shadows, and had given her a new life at his side.

Damian had noticed how she had changed in five years of marriage, but she wondered whether he really understood how much she'd changed. Of the impulsive, emotional adolescent she'd once been, almost nothing was left. The cool, poised woman who was now called Mrs Kirby Waterford was light years away from the weeping, bewildered eighteen-year-old called Kirby

Bryant who had been so tragically infatuated with a man who could never, ever love her.

She heard the deep note of a car's engine approaching the house up the drive. She knew it was Damian, and desperately tried to shake away the mood her painful memories had brought. She needed to have all her defences at the ready in order to face Damian right now.

She waited until she heard the front doorbell chime. Then she rose, took a deep breath, and went to let him in.

Damian was wearing a rough sheepskin jacket, the perfect attire for his rugged frame. The fleecy collar made a frame for the splendidly handsome face that smiled down at her.

'Nice little shack you have here,' he commented as he came in. 'You must get a good view of Braythorpe—when the Yorkshire mist lifts.'

'Don't you get mists in London?' she asked him sarcastically.

'Not like this,' he replied, closing the door on the swirling white nimbus. He shrugged off the sheepskin jacket, revealing that he wore clothes similar to hers beneath—denims that hugged his lean hips and powerful thighs, and a chunky black sweater that was amply filled by his broad shoulders.

He surveyed her. 'My God. You look almost like Kirby Bryant again instead of Mrs Keith Waterford.'

She folded her arms belligerently. 'You mean I look a mess?'

'I mean you look delicious,' he smiled. 'Tweed suits and silk blouses are all very well in their place, but...' He turned and glanced around the spacious hallway. 'So this is the Lodge. Not bad. Must cost a fortune to heat.'

She led him to the drawing-room, where the fire was crackling. 'I expect you have a palatial residence of your own somewhere in Hampstead or St John's Wood?'

'I have a bachelor flat in the West End,' he replied. He studied the handsome Victorian furnishings of the drawing-room. 'Very elegant. Very dignified. But doesn't all the elegance and dignity suffocate you sometimes?'

'I cope,' she said drily.

'Do you?'

'Perfectly. I'm not the naïve little girl whose heart you broke six years ago.'

'Did I break your heart?' he asked in a soft voice that gave her goosebumps.

'In any case,' she said, not answering his question, 'your fiancée Wendy doesn't strike me as the sort of girl who'd fit into a bachelor flat in the West End. So you'd better start reconciling yourself to that palatial house in Hampstead . . . *darling Damian*.'

She had tilted her oval face up at him challengingly. Unexpectedly, he reached out, and touched the lustrous chestnut curls that framed her face. His voice was husky. 'I'd give a lot to hear you say that as though you meant it, Kirby.'

His touch was so gentle. Suddenly, she was drowning in those slate-blue eyes. She felt her heart turn over inside her breast, her legs becoming weak. She shut her eyes for a moment, then turned away. 'I've asked you not to flirt with me, Damian,' she said through clenched teeth. 'It was never a game to me, not even six years ago. Far less now.' She pressed her damp palms to her denims. 'Now,' she went on, trying to sound normal, 'can I make you a cup of tea or coffee? Or would you prefer something stronger?'

Damian smiled. 'Would you have any whisky about the place?'

She poured him a single malt, and herself a smaller version of the same drink. She hated strong spirits, but she was hoping the alcohol would lend strength to her weak legs.

He toasted her silently, then gestured to the sofa in front of the fire. 'Let's sit down and talk, Kirby.'

She cleared the pile of magazines to make a space for them. He took them from her, and glanced at the glossy covers. 'You read a lot of these. The occupation of a lonely woman?'

She flushed. 'I like to keep up with the fashions.'

'Who for?'

'For myself,' she retorted. 'And for the men in my life. They do seem to notice what I wear.'

'The men in your life?' he echoed.

'There's no shortage,' she said defiantly.

'No,' he agreed. 'There never was. I used to notice that.'

'My memories are rather the other way round,' she replied pointedly. 'It was you who enjoyed breaking hearts. But we're not here to discuss ancient history.'

Damian glanced at her in amusement. Her full, soft mouth was compressed into a determined line, and her normally gentle eyes were narrowed defensively. 'All right. Down to business.' They sat down in opposite corners of the sofa, facing each other within touching distance. He drank, then put the glass down. 'Well, I've spoken to both Sir Malcolm Denison and Roderick Braithwaite, and you're right. Both are making a determined bid for the chairmanship of Waterford Electronics. On paper, Sir Malcolm Denison is the more serious contender—he holds a lot of shares. Not as many as you, of course. Keith was careful to retain enough of the stock to make a take-over bid difficult, and that stock has passed to you. But Denison holds enough to make a lot of trouble if he chose to sell out to another company which was, shall we say, strong-minded about the direction Waterford Electronics should take.'

Kirby nodded. 'You said "on paper".'

'Yes. Braithwaite holds fewer shares. But he does have a very thorough knowledge of Waterford Electronics, and if he takes that to a rival company he could do you a lot of damage. Also, he's apparently a good manager, and would be a loss to the firm.'

She studied Damian as he outlined the position. He had always been a magnificently good-looking man. Now that he was in his mid-thirties, maturity was adding an even more potent dimension to his allure.

And he had something else. Sex appeal. Not all handsome men had it—no more than all beautiful women. He had charisma, that almost electric aura that surrounded many very successful men. It seemed to crackle in the air, smoulder in those grey-blue eyes. It would have made him a wildly attractive man even if he'd been ordinary-looking. As it was, the combination was devastating. Damian was quite simply, she thought dreamily, the most attractive man she would ever know.

'Are you listening?' he challenged. 'Don't go to sleep on me, Kirby.'

'Sorry,' she said, sitting up straighter. 'I was concentrating, really.'

'You looked as though you were dreaming of the hills of heaven,' he commented. He ran his lean fingers through his thick, dark hair, raking it back from his temples. The crow's-feet that were starting to deepen at the corners of his eyes creased into a wry smile. 'Up till now,' he went on, 'I get the impression that Roderick Braithwaite and Sir Malcolm Denison have more or less cancelled each other out. Am I right?'

She nodded. 'There's always been antagonism between the two men. It's more a matter of character than opinion, because both of them—in my woman's-eye view, at least—have got the same ruthless attitude towards Waterford Electronics. You know what I mean.'

'Yes,' he agreed. 'They've both got very definite ideas about the future of the company.'

'Since Keith died, they've been clashing horns almost constantly. It disrupts the board meetings terribly, and I'm worn out with it.' She gave Damian a sad shrug. 'I'm the one who takes the final brunt of the collision. In the ten months since Keith's death I've learned one lesson very thoroughly.'

'What's that?'

'Being chairman of Waterford Electronics means taking uncomplaining responsibility for everything nasty that happens, whether it's my fault or not. And now I have an ominous feeling that something nasty is about to happen.'

'Your ominous feeling is right,' Damian assented. 'Roderick Braithwaite and Sir Malcolm Denison may be about to join forces.'

'Oh, no! How did you find that out?'

'I've had a lot of experience in uncovering company plots,' he pointed out drily. 'It was inevitable. If they start working together, instead of clashing horns, as you put it, they feel they may be able to successfully challenge your authority. They think they can get enough of the rest of the board to go their way, and do what they want with the company.' He surveyed Kirby's dismayed expression. 'All this will likely come out in next Friday's board meeting.'

'Oh, my God,' she sighed, resting her head in her hand.

'That's the bad news.'

She looked up quickly. 'Is there good news?'

'There might be,' he nodded.

'You've found a way of stopping them?'

'Oh, yes. But you may not like it.'

'Try me,' she invited quietly.

He grinned, showing his beautiful white teeth. 'Not so fast. I'm starving. Got anything to eat in this château?'

'There's some cottage pie,' she said doubtfully. 'But I suppose that's too unsophisticated for your tastes...'

'Cottage pie sounds perfect.'

'If you wait here, I'll bring a tray.'

'Nonsense. We can eat in the kitchen. I'll come and help.'

She led him to the kitchen. It was a typically spacious Victorian kitchen, the original copper pots and pans still gleaming on the walls, though all the appliances were, naturally, modern.

Damian looked around quizzically. 'I thought places like this only existed in TV costume dramas.'

'So did I, until I got married.' She took the cottage pie out of the fridge, and removed the cling-film.

He inspected it. 'All your own work?'

'Actually, Mrs Carstairs made it for me.'

'Mrs Carstairs?'

'The housekeeper.'

He nodded. 'Of course. No doubt there are a bevy of chambermaids and footmen, too.'

'There are two girls who help Mrs Carstairs,' she replied.

'All just to wait on little old you?'

'A big house like this takes a lot of running,' she said stiffly. 'Of course, there was more point to the staff when Keith was alive. We entertained a lot. I could manage without them now. But why should I do them out of a job just because I've suffered?'

'A fine sentiment.'

'I'm a sentimental person,' she said shortly, catching the mockery in his words. She put the cottage pie in the microwave oven, and laid two places at the pine kitchen table where she was accustomed to eat these days. Damian watched her, his smile more in those slate-blue eyes than on the chiselled mouth. 'And you needn't worry about the meal,' she told him. 'Mrs Carstairs is an excellent cook.'

'I suppose you've never had to soil a dainty finger since the day you married Keith?'

'Mum taught me to cook, as you very well know.' She couldn't help a counter-gibe. 'And your dear Wendy? Can she boil an egg?'

'Not on your life,' he grinned. 'Wendy can't even use a can-opener.'

'Poor you.' She turned away to hide her pleasure at hearing there was *something* the perfect Wendy couldn't do. 'Should I open a bottle of wine?'

'Naturally. Shall I go down to the cellar and fetch madam a bottle of the Mouton Rothschild '32?'

She smiled despite herself. 'That won't be necessary. I have some good Spanish Rioja right here.' She handed him the corkscrew. 'You can do the honours.'

Ten minutes later, they were sitting down to the hot food opposite each other. 'You're right,' Damian said appreciatively. 'Your Mrs Carstairs is a good cook.'

'Cooking isn't really a part of her duties. She just does it out of kindness now and then.'

He filled her glass. 'Would it be classed as flirting,' he asked, 'if I said how much I've missed you in these past six years, Kirby?'

'Perhaps not flirting,' she replied, 'but certainly a lie. You haven't given me a thought since you left Braythorpe.'

'You're wrong,' Damian said gently. 'I don't think a day has gone by when I haven't thought of you.'

Her appetite had suddenly gone, and she could hardly touch the food. She forced herself to sound flippant. 'One thought a day in six years? That means you've had two thousand one hundred and ninety thoughts of me.'

'You always had a quick brain for maths,' he smiled. 'But you've left out the leap year. Two thousand one hundred and ninety-one. And you?'

'And me—what?'

His eyes held hers. 'How often have you thought of me?'

'I'm afraid my mental powers aren't up to that calculation. You'd need a super-computer.'

And immediately she bitterly regretted giving him that mortifying insight into her heart. The whisky and the wine must have loosened her tongue disastrously for her to have spoken so foolishly!

Damian was studying her intently. 'Did you love Keith?' he asked.

'What sort of question is that?' she said angrily. 'Of course I did!'

'I think it's a fair question—when you've just admitted that you never stopped thinking of me.'

'I didn't say my thoughts were kind ones,' she retorted, her flush deepening. 'For all you know I might have cursed you every time!'

'You might,' he conceded. 'But I don't think you did, somehow.'

'Your vanity was always colossal,' she said nastily. 'Let's get back to business, Damian. What's this master-plan you have to save Waterford Electronics for me?'

'I haven't worked out all the details yet,' he replied easily, re-filling her glass. 'I'd prefer to wait until I have before explaining it to you.'

'And how long will that be?'

'Have patience. Not your strong point, I know.'

'I have great patience!' she exclaimed.

'Have you? You rushed into marriage with a singular lack of it, I thought.'

'Indeed!' she snapped back. 'Would you rather I'd spent the past six years crying in that summer-house? I had a life to lead, Damian. And, as I've just told you, I loved Keith very much. He was a wonderful husband and, a bare year after his death, I really don't think you have the right to—the right to——'

She choked on the lump that rose up in her throat, no matter how hard she fought it down. Furiously determined not to break down in front of Damian, she pushed her chair back and left the table. She walked quickly into the hall, and stood there with clenched fists, taking shaky breaths to try to control her anger and grief.

Damn him! And damn her own vulnerability! When was she ever going to learn any sense as far as Damian Holt was concerned?

She felt his presence behind her, but did not turn.

His hands took her shoulders gently, then ran down her arms in a slow caress. 'I'm sorry,' she heard his deep voice murmur. 'I was a pig. I'll never say that again.'

'You were right,' she replied in a tight voice. 'You haven't changed at all, Damian.'

'No.' Her heart lurched as she felt his arms slide around her. 'Nothing has changed,' he whispered. He drew her close against his warm body. His mouth was buried in the soft tangle of her chestnut hair. 'Nothing,' he repeated.

Kirby found she was shaking. She wanted to break free of this wonderful, terrible embrace; but all she could do was lean against him, weak as water.

Damian's hands caressed her tenderly. 'Nobody said this was going to be easy,' he murmured. 'I warned you it might be difficult.'

'You didn't say it might be impossible,' she whispered.

He turned her around to face him. Her oval face looked up at him defencelessly, her eyes dark with emotion. 'Nothing's impossible, Kirby,' he said. He studied her from under hooded lids. 'You're so very beautiful,' he told her, his fingertips trailing down the smooth skin of her cheek. 'Your skin glows like ivory. Cool, pale, smooth.'

And then he cupped her face in his hands, and brushed her lips with his.

His kiss was little more than a touch. The warmth of his mouth was against hers for a moment, no more. But she felt the reaction sweep across her skin in a wave of goose-flesh, and her eyes closed helplessly. He whispered her name, and kissed her again, his arms drawing her close to him.

This time the kiss was not just a delicate brushing of velvety lips. This time his kiss contained passion. Like the kisses he'd given her six years ago, in the darkness of the garden, when the miracle had seemed to be happening.

Kirby's lips parted under the gentle onslaught. She felt him take the softness of her lower lip between his white teeth, biting almost cruelly, until she whimpered. Immediately, his tongue sought forgiveness, tracing the shape of her mouth, meeting the sensitive tip of her own tongue.

It was as though she had no control over her own body. Her slender arms crept around his neck of their own accord, pulling his head to her, inviting him to kiss her harder, more fiercely...

Damian's hand had slid under the soft angora wool, and his palm was caressing her ribs. The aroused condition of her skin made his touch almost a torment as it drifted slowly towards the curve of her breasts...

Kirby was a petite woman, and she seldom wore a bra unless it was strictly necessary. Already the naked skin of her breasts was tightening unbearably at his approaching caress. She could not bite back her moan of reaction as his hand cupped the gentle swell of her breast, stroking the satin-smooth skin tantalisingly as his tongue plundered the deep inner secrets of her mouth.

It was happening again. Her miracle. As it had happened on her eighteenth birthday. Now, as then, she could feel Damian's hunger for her, could feel the hardness of his loins against hers. Now, as long ago, she heard her own husky whisper of desire at his touch. Felt the pressure of their mutual need, like the great thrust of a lake against the dam wall, longing to burst free, to explode into foaming life.

Would she, as then, feel the unbearable agony of rejection?

She tore her mouth away from his. 'Don't!' she gasped. 'Damian, stop!'

'Why?' he demanded, his voice rough with arousal. He smiled down at her with smoky eyes. 'We've both ached for this ever since we first set eyes on each other again.'

'No!' she whispered in violent denial.

'Then if you haven't, I have.' His palm caressed the erect peaks of her nipples, concentrating them into twin stars of erotic passion. His very gentleness was a cruel aphrodisiac. 'I know your body so well,' he said, his mouth caressing her eyelids, her temples, the arching line of her throat. 'I've thought of it so many times over the past six years. Remembering its sweetness, its delicacy. Remembering the taste of your kiss...'

'And the taste of my tears,' she choked. 'You bastard!' She ran her trembling palms across the hard muscles of his shoulders, up his neck. Damian's hair was crisp and thick as she knotted her fingers in its darkness. The smell of his hair was intoxicating, achingly familiar. It brought back all her passionate love for him in a devastating wave.

She pulled on his hair fiercely, drawing his mouth back to hers. He kissed her with burning intensity, his palms roaming across the smooth skin of her back, pulling her against the thrust of desire at his loins.

'God, I want you, Kirby,' he said raggedly.

'Do you?' Sanity was making its way through the swirling mist of her passion. Sanity—and a sense of disbelief at her own loss of reason.

She stepped back from Damian, the blood roaring in her ears. 'Well, I want you, too, Damian. So now you know.'

And she swung her palm with all her force at his face.

He could probably have parried or avoided the blow. But he made no move to avert it, and the slap crashed into his cheek with considerable force. Kirby stood facing him, her whole body rigid with tension and emotion, her palm stinging. There had been a great deal of pent-up emotion in that slap.

He met her eyes. 'All right,' he said softly. 'I deserved that. I earned it six years ago. You've paid me back, Kirby. And now can we leave the past behind, and start again?'

'Not a chance,' she flashed at him. 'Not a chance in hell!'

She turned on her heel, and strode back to the kitchen. She was in a towering rage—with him, with herself. She snatched up the plates in shaking hands, and started scraping the half-eaten meals—she was finished eating, even if he wasn't—into the dustbin.

Damian's voice was gentle behind her. 'Kirby, take it easy.'

'No, I will *not* take it easy,' she snapped. She threw the cutlery and crockery into the sink, and started the washing up, not caring whether the glass and china broke or not. The intense desire that he had aroused in her body was still swirling in her veins, but now it only added energy to her anger. 'I said you hadn't changed. I was wrong. You've grown even more despicable!'

'All because I kissed you?'

'Yes! All because you kissed me!' She slammed the plates down on to the rack to drain. 'Is that why you said you'd help me, Damian?' she asked through clenched teeth. 'So you could do that to me all over again?'

'No,' he replied quietly. 'There's a difference. This time I wouldn't have stopped.'

'Oh, thank you for that compliment,' she said bitterly, turning to face him. 'What am I to you, Damian? The one that got away? Some unfinished business that you came back to conclude?'

'No, Kirby. It isn't like that.'

'What's it like, then? A movie you had to walk out of? A book you haven't finished yet? Can't you resist seeing how the story ends?' She seized a cloth, and dried her soapy hands. 'I let you destroy my life once before, Damian. I'll never let you do that again. Never. Do you understand me?'

She could see the mark of her palm in Damian's cheek, a dull flush on the tanned skin. 'I understand that you still love me,' he replied in a calm voice.

Kirby's eyes blurred with tears. 'So it's power you want.'

He shook his head slowly. 'That's not what I want, Kirby.'

'You do. You want reassurance that your spell is fatal. You want me to tell you that, despite everything, despite five years of marriage to Keith, despite what you did to me, I'm still your creature. Your pawn, to toy with and manipulate as you please. Well, I'm *not*,' she asserted grimly. 'The last time you knew me I was a virgin. Now I'm a widow. I was eighteen in that summer-house. I'm a twenty-four-year-old woman now. I'm nobody's toy, Damian. Not even yours.'

'I never wanted you to be my toy,' he said quietly, his deep eyes fixed on her face. 'I tried to tear you out of my heart six years ago. But something of me came away, and stayed with you. I've never got it back, Kirby. I don't think I ever will.'

'Ask Wendy Catchpole to give it to you,' she retorted savagely.

'If you think Wendy means a fraction of what you do to me, then you're a fool, Kirby.'

'My God,' she said icily, 'I didn't think you'd stoop to that.'

'It's the truth.'

'And yet you're going to marry her?'

'The marriage is extremely convenient for both parties. A lot of money is involved. But I don't love Wendy. And she certainly doesn't love me.'

Kirby's heart was pounding against her breast so painfully that she felt ill. 'What am I supposed to say to that?' she whispered.

'Nothing. I'm not asking you to say anything. Yet.'

She laughed painfully. 'And when did you decide that you cared so much about *me*?'

'A long, long time ago,' he replied, his eyes never leaving hers. 'But I was reminded again, last Friday night, as soon as I set eyes on you.' He touched his cheek and smiled slightly, a softer light in the slate-blue eyes. 'You pack a wallop, Kirby.'

'At least I fight fair,' she said in a low voice. 'You go for the jugular, Damian.'

'I mean business,' he agreed.

The anger was draining out of her, to be replaced by utter exhaustion. She looked at the mark on his face, and felt a pang of remorse. 'Did I really hurt you?'

'Damn right you did.'

She stepped forward, and laid her palm against his cheek where she had struck him. 'I'm sorry,' she whispered, her brown eyes moist. 'But you did deserve it.'

'I know.' He took her hand, and kissed the knuckles. She felt the melting rush of desire all over again. He sensed it, too, and drew her forward.

But she pulled away from him, shaking her head so sharply that the glossy curls of her hair rippled. 'No, Damian. I meant what I said. I'm never going to let you make a fool of me again. I'm sorry that you and Wendy don't love one another. But it really doesn't affect me. Because I don't love you any more, Damian. I got over you a long, long time ago.'

He studied her eyes, then smiled. 'Good,' he said simply. 'I'm glad. That means we can start with a clean slate.'

'What do you mean,' she demanded, 'start with a clean slate?'

'I mean it's late, and I have to go.'

'You still haven't told me what your great plan is. Or were you just playing another kind of game with me when you said that?'

'No, I wasn't playing any kind of game. The plan can wait a while, though. I'll tell you everything before the board meeting, don't worry. Thanks for the meal, Kirby. And everything else.'

She followed him into the hall. He slung the heavy sheepskin jacket over one broad shoulder, and smiled down at her. 'How long has it been since you went to Sovereign Force?'

'Years,' she replied automatically. 'Why?'

'You said you missed riding these days. We'll hire a couple of horses on Thursday morning, and ride up to Sovereign Force together. How about it?'

'Damian, I hardly think——'

'And on the ride,' he cut in smoothly, 'I'll tell you about my idea for saving your company.'

Kirby hesitated unhappily. 'All right,' she said at last. 'If you really insist.'

'Excellent,' he purred. 'In the meantime, I want you to get some papers ready for me.' He explained what they were, and she agreed to obtain them from the company records.

Kirby walked him to the door. He pulled on his jacket, looking out into the thick mist. 'What a climate,' he smiled. 'You're like the damsel in the tower in some fairy-tale. Waiting for the white knight to come and rescue you from the dragons.'

Before she could avoid his lips, he had stooped and kissed her firmly on the mouth.

Then he was walking down the stairs into the mist. An engine growled into life, and headlights blazed, turning the mist into a huge star-burst. She saw the dim outline of his Porsche swing around on the drive, and thought she caught the wave of his arm. Then he was gone.

Kirby went inside, closed the door, and leaned against it feeling utterly drained. How long ago had she been congratulating herself on how much she'd matured, on how far she'd grown away from the impulsive, emotional adolescent she'd once been? Two hours? It felt like an eternity.

She closed her eyes, and saw Damian's face wearing that veiled, mocking smile. Felt his touch on the secret desires of her body. Remembered the husky whisper of his voice. And knew that when Damian touched her she was no longer the cool, poised woman called Mrs Kirby Waterford. She was a lot closer to the bewildered girl called Kirby Bryant who had sobbed in the darkness, long ago, as her world had come crashing down around her ears.

CHAPTER SIX

KIRBY went in to the factory the next morning, as she usually did two or three times a week. Somewhat to her surprise, Roderick Braithwaite was in his office. He looked up at her as she paused in his doorway. His expression was cold.

'Good morning, Roderick,' she said easily. 'Nice to see you. I thought you wouldn't be coming in for a week or two?' She walked into Keith's office, next door to his.

She heard his chair scrape as he rose to follow her.

'Funny coincidence,' he greeted her abruptly. 'I was just talking about your whiz-kid cousin the other night, wasn't I?'

'What's the coincidence?' she asked innocently.

Roderick's face was grim. 'I had a visit from him yesterday. He's up from London, it seems. Full of questions and queries about Waterford Electronics. And he's subjected Malcolm Denison to the same kind of interrogation as well! Like a damned wolf, sniffing round the tent! I don't like it at all, Kirby. You had no call to go fetching outsiders into our little squabble——'

She gave Roderick Braithwaite a dry look from intelligent brown eyes. 'Would you call it a little squabble, Roderick? To me it sounded like an ultimatum followed by an unconditional resignation.'

He looked taken aback for a moment. 'We both got emotional, Kirby——'

'*You* got emotional.' Kirby pressed the intercom on her desk to call her secretary. 'Marie? Could you bring in two coffees, please?'

'Yes, Mrs Waterford,' came the tinny response. Kirby settled into the chair beneath the portrait of Keith, and looked at Roderick. 'Do I take it you now wish to withdraw your resignation?'

'I haven't even tendered it yet, damn it all,' he said, his face darkening.

'You didn't come to work yesterday. Or the day before.'

'Now, look.' He sank into the chair opposite her desk. 'I might have got a bit emotional the other night, I admit. I was wrong to say anything about resigning.' His eyes flickered from side to side. 'But my pride was hurt, Kirby. That's why I didn't turn up this week. It isn't every day a man proposes to a woman he thinks the world of, and when he gets turned down flat—well, it makes him see red. Now I've apologised for all that. Can't we sort out our differences without the likes of Damian Holt coming into it?'

'Our differences are a little too wide for easy solutions. You demanded the chairmanship of Waterford Electronics, and I said that was impossible. It seems to me you must either accept that, Roderick, unpalatable as it may be, or do as you threatened, and look for better fortune elsewhere.'

Marie, the office secretary, brought in coffee and biscuits at that point, silencing whatever retort Roderick had been building up to. Kirby waited until Marie was leaving, and timed her next statement to cut him off again.

'As for what you call "fetching in outsiders", it was you who threatened to take confidential information about this company to Integrated Circuits. All I did was ask Damian Holt for some advice.'

'Advice!' Roderick snorted. 'Aye, and you know what kind of *advice* Damian Holt likes to give. "Make yourselves nice and small, my lambs, so I can swallow you whole!"'

Kirby had to hide a smile. 'I doubt whether Damian Holt is interested in Waterford Electronics.'

'Then you don't know anything about business,' Roderick replied rudely. 'This is *exactly* the size company that the Holt Corporation likes to take over. And, since you've no doubt told him a very exaggerated version of our trivial internal difficulties, he probably thinks this is a perfect opportunity for him to move in and——' He took a deep breath. 'Let me give you a little warning, Kirby. If you're thinking of selling Waterford Electronics off to the Holt Corporation, just because I dropped a few comments, you've lost your marbles. We'd be better off sorting out our little problems without benefit of the likes of *that*. Asset-stripping isn't a pretty sight, I assure you.'

She was secretly amused by Roderick's passion. So he thought she was planning to sell out to the Holt Corporation! He was too stupid to see that she would never dream of doing such a thing, but at least it had shaken him up considerably. 'All I'm doing at the moment is asking Damian Holt's advice,' she said calmly. 'And it's certainly not exclusively to do with you. The problem is bigger than any one board member. I don't want to spend the rest of my life fighting off bids for the company, Roderick. I've asked him to find a way of making sure that this company keeps trading in a way that my husband would have approved of—without the need for constant policing.'

'But that's exactly what I would do,' Roderick snapped. 'I respected Keith, Kirby. He was like a younger brother to me! I only want to see Waterford Electronics carry on in the way he would have wanted!'

She gave him a cool look. 'Is that what you meant last week when you said you were going to pull Waterford Electronics out of the Dark Ages? ''Bigger and faster profits than it's ever seen before''? That hardly sounds like Keith.'

'You're twisting my words——'

'I'm simply repeating them. Keith ran this company for the good of the whole town, Roderick, not just as a means of making fast profits. And I'm not going to give in to anyone who wants to pervert what Keith wanted.'

Roderick was staring at her in a hostile silence. 'You're still sweet on him, aren't you?' he grated abruptly.

'What?'

'Damian Holt. Your heart-throb of long ago. Why should he be the one to be called in? How did you come to be lunching with him at expensive restaurants?'

'Word gets around fast in this town,' she said tersely.

'You're still soft on him, Kirby.' Roderick sneered crudely. 'You sit there under Keith's portrait and accuse me of being unfaithful to his ideals. Well, he isn't even twelve months dead, and you're already thinking of selling out to the man who dropped you in the gutter, where Keith picked you up. Who's being unfaithful? You or me?'

'How dare you?' Kirby said shakily, her face drained of colour. 'How *dare* you speak so coarsely and unjustly to me?'

Roderick rose abruptly, and walked to the window, looking out over the angled roofs of the assembly-line.

'All right, I'm sorry,' he muttered. 'You're right. That was uncalled-for.'

'Getting personal is not going to solve anything.' The pain in her heart was sharp and bitter.

He looked at her gloomily. 'How much is he offering for your shares?'

'He hasn't made any offers yet,' she replied.

'Bear this in mind—between us, Sir Malcolm Denison and I could probably give you a fair price. We don't have Damian Holt's financial resources. But we *were* Keith's friends, and——'

'I'll let you know about any decisions I make at the board meeting next week,' she said firmly. 'I don't want to say any more at this stage.'

He glanced at her sharply, then shrugged. 'All right. I'd better go down to the shop-floor and do some work.' He went out, leaving his coffee untasted.

Kirby sat motionless behind Keith's desk, feeling the pain swelling inside her, hearing the crude words echoing in her head.

The man who dropped you in the gutter, where Keith picked you up.

It took her ten minutes to recover enough to rise, go to the locked filing cabinet in the corner, and start locating the papers that Damian had requested she have ready for him.

She felt weak and shaken. Guilt hung over her like a thundercloud. As if Damian hadn't scarred her enough, she had endured guilt for the full five years of her marriage—a secret, consuming remorse that she didn't love Keith enough. That she had loved another man more than she loved her husband.

And then Keith had died, and there was no way she could ever make it up to him, and the guilt had remained, grown inward, becoming more painful than ever.

That clumsy blow from Roderick Braithwaite had hurt more than he could have imagined.

You're still sweet on him, aren't you? Who's being unfaithful? You or me?

Horrible, unfair words. Yet Roderick's accusations contained a kernel of truth. Damian had started haunting her, the way she'd known he would. Her mind was full of thoughts of him.

Last night she had dreamed of him, the kind of dream she hadn't had for years, so intense and sweet that she had awoken, her pillow wet with forbidden tears.

She'd had to lie there, lashing her mind with reminders. Remember what he did to you. Remember what he has become. Remember that he's going to marry another woman.

That last thought had done it. Sickened by his callous attitude towards marriage, she'd managed to chase her dream back into its lair. For a while...

Although Sovereign Force was one of the most beautiful spots in the whole of Braydale, its inaccessibility meant that few people, apart from riders and the most determined hikers, ever got there. 'Force' was an old north word for a waterfall, and the Force itself was a spectacular ravine, where the Bray spilled some forty feet down to a pool below.

But the only feasible route there was an uphill climb of several miles along the course of the river through alternating rock and moorland. It was hard going, even for the big, strong horses Kirby and Damian had hired on Thursday morning.

After two hours, they halted to let the horses rest a little. Kirby turned in her saddle, and looked back the way they had come. The craggy moors stretched down in mauve sheets towards the valley below where Braythorpe nestled snugly. A sky pregnant with rain hung heavily overhead, lending a sombre grandeur to the view.

The wind swept Kirby's hair away from the oval of her face, and she looked up at the clouds. 'I hope it doesn't rain for a while.' They were both wearing rugged outdoor jackets against the threatening weather, but there was still an hour's ride to the Force, and a three-hour ride back down to Braythorpe.

'Beautiful, isn't it?' Damian said, staring down the valley.

She glanced at him. 'So you do still feel something?'

'Of course I do. My roots will always be here, Kirby. There's nothing I can do about that.'

'Don't tell me you sit in your glass tower in London dreaming of the moors?' she mocked.

'Sometimes I do exactly that,' he replied. 'There are times when I'd give a lot to see this view.'

She patted her horse's neck. 'Look your fill,' she advised him drily. 'I doubt whether you'll get up here very often after your marriage. Wendy didn't strike me as having any particular fondness for North Yorkshire.'

'You think she's going to run my life?' he asked, amused.

'She positively reeks of authority. But you obviously have few illusions about one another. No doubt she won't be too terribly shocked when you go on little escapades—geographical or otherwise.'

Damian laughed. 'No, she probably won't be too shocked.'

Kirby could not stop distaste from hardening her soft mouth. 'How did you propose to her, darling Damian? Did you suggest a merger? Or was it more of an incorporation?'

'Oh, it just came out. During one of those...appropriate moments.'

'What moments are those?'

'You're not a virgin any more,' he said composedly. 'I'm sure you know what I mean.'

She flushed angrily. 'Well, I'm glad there's *some* warmth between you and your fiancée.'

'Warmth?' He appeared to consider the word. 'No, I wouldn't call it warmth. Sex doesn't have to be warm, Kirby. Sometimes it's nothing more than...a muscle relaxant.'

'I really don't want to know,' she said tightly, wheeling her horse round.

'Then what did you ask for?'

She didn't answer, just urged her horse back into a walk. His mount fell into step beside hers as they continued the ride uphill. She rode in silence for a while, emotion churning inside her. At last she couldn't help bursting out, 'I'm sickened, Damian! I never dreamed that you'd become so calculating. I realise that success means a great deal to you. But to contemplate such a cold, mercenary marriage...it's obscene!'

'I'd prefer to call it practical,' he replied. 'Wendy and I each have something the other wants. Why should it disturb you if we're not hypocritical about love?'

'Because marriage is more than just a—just a combining of interests! I was married for five years, Damian, and this is one area where I know more than you do.' She turned a passionate face to him. 'I've got nothing against Wendy Catchpole. When I met her, I thought she was the perfect wife for you. But if you don't love her, for God's sake don't marry her.'

'Moral indignation puts a lovely colour into your cheeks, Kirby,' Damian said, still smiling. 'Why shouldn't I marry Wendy?'

'Because one day one of you might meet someone you *do* love,' she told him in a low voice, 'and then you'll understand what you've done to each other.'

'Oh, I don't think that eventuality need concern us,' he replied easily. 'Our marriage will have plenty of scope for what you call "escapades". Neither of us is going to play policeman on the other.'

'Love is never an *escapade*, Damian. You can't tell it when to happen. You can't call it off when you feel like it. And being married to one person when you love another is a terrible fate.'

He raised one eyebrow. 'Are you speaking from personal experience there?'

'No,' she said shortly. 'My marriage to Keith was very happy. And, as I told you the other night, my infatuation with you vanished a long, long time ago. But I do still care about you as…a friend. As a friend, I'm telling you that marriage without love can only ever be a torment.'

'And yet,' he said, silkily dropping the net around her, 'the other day you were telling me you're seriously considering Roderick Braithwaite's proposal…even though you admit you wouldn't be marrying for love.'

'Oh, that…'

'Yes, that. Explain this apparent inconsistency, Mrs Waterford.'

'I can't. Except to repeat the old saying, "Do as I say, not as I do."'

'I'll bear your advice in mind,' he said with gentle mockery. 'Now, save your breath for the climb.'

They reached Sovereign Force at noon, and could hear the rumble of the waterfall as they tethered the horses. They walked through the thicket of trees, the sound of the water growing to a roar of thunder as they approached.

It was a spectacular sight. They had emerged at the foot of a tall cliff which interrupted the river's flow. The water poured from high above where they stood, exploding down the jagged rock-face in a violent succession of cataracts, the foam stark white against the black of the rock. The deep pool below was continually roiling and swirling with the cascade that poured into it. Further along, overhung by trees, the pool narrowed to resume the course of the Bray down through the dale.

The clamour of the water was so loud that they could not hear each other speak, but Kirby felt Damian's strong fingers twine around hers. She held on tightly to his hand, revelling in the elemental energy of the scene. 'Force' was the perfect word for this phenomenon. She recalled, with almost painful clarity, her emotions when Damian had kissed her. Then, too, she had felt a wild, primal force at work inside her, straining to explode into life, as this waterfall was doing now.

Her eyes followed the waterfall down to the dark pool beneath. And there, she thought sombrely, was the whirlpool, waiting to suck her down. The water spun and whirled, dragging the river's floating debris of leaves and twigs deep into the unknown depths. She shuddered at the thought of the icy black chasm beneath the water.

Damian, mistaking her shiver for cold, drew her close, his arm sliding around her waist. She was achingly aware of his strong body against hers, of his protective warmth. They stood watching the cascade together for a long while. For a moment, the clouds parted overhead, and a few silvery rays struck down into the ravine. The mist was suddenly a dance of rainbows, and Kirby marvelled at the opalescent beauty of it. Like water-nymphs, she thought, exulting in the raw energy of their haunt. Then the light dulled, and the rainbows faded back to black and white.

They turned, and walked back to the horses.

'I'm so glad we came,' she said, as soon as they could hear one another speak. 'I'd forgotten how magnificent it is.'

'It has a pagan beauty,' he agreed. 'They say the Druids used to worship there. I can believe it.'

'So can I.'

Damian unhitched the saddle-bag he had been carrying, and gave it to Kirby. They'd brought a simple picnic with them, and they were both hungry after the exercise. They spread the blankets out under the shelter of a tree, and sat down where they could enjoy the grandeur of the view, with the distant reverberation of the Force as a musical backdrop.

Kirby investigated the saddle-bag, producing a bottle of champagne, some cold chicken, a crusty farmhouse loaf, and plenty of fruit. She inspected the champagne dubiously. 'This is probably primed to go off like a grenade after the shaking it's had.'

'I'm too thirsty to care,' Damian said. He took the bottle, and prised the cork out with strong fingers. It exploded, as Kirby had predicted, in a spray to rival the waterfall; but once the foam had subsided there was enough of the golden liquid to fill their plastic cups. 'Here's to you,' Damian smiled, toasting her.

'And to you,' she echoed, lifting her cup. The champagne was deliciously bubbly, the perfect drink for this moment. Despite the threatening sky, Kirby felt a sense of pure happiness settle around her heart. She was sitting in one of the most beautiful spots in England, alone with the man she loved most in all the world. What else mattered?

They tucked into the food without ceremony. 'So,' Damian said, slicing the chicken, 'how's your week been, Mrs Waterford?'

'Up and down, Mr Holt.' She told him about her encounter with Roderick Braithwaite the other day—excluding Roderick's cruel parting comment. 'He hasn't said much since then,' she concluded, 'but he's obviously worried about you. And when I saw Malcolm Denison, he also asked a few pertinent questions about your involvement.' She smiled with wicked amusement. 'They both seem convinced that I'm about to sell Waterford Electronics to you.'

'Do they?'

'They're worried sick. Roderick called you a wolf, sniffing round the tent. And Malcolm said something about corporate raiders and boardroom pirates. Is that what you are, Damian—a boardroom pirate?'

'I've been known to buy the odd company. But I'm not in the corporate raiding business.'

'Well, you've certainly got Roderick and Malcolm on the run. For intelligent men they really have a very limited outlook. As if I'd dream of selling Waterford Electronics to you! The whole point of the exercise is to keep the company in safe hands.'

'And you don't think my hands are safe?' he asked casually, refilling her cup with champagne.

'No safer than Roderick or Malcolm's, that's for sure,' she laughed. 'If I can't trust them, how could I ever trust *you*?'

'I'm offended,' he said with mock-affront.

'After the little speech you gave me on the way up here?' she snorted. 'A man who would marry for money is hardly the right person to trust to be altruistic in business. What about those poor fishermen whose river you poisoned? And the boy who died in the air crash? No, Damian. You don't have a very good record on human rights. In fact, I couldn't ever believe you capable of any kind of altruistic action at all!'

Damian lay back, biting into an apple. He surveyed her with lazy eyes. 'Your pals Roderick and Sir Malcolm aren't entirely off-course, you know,' he said. 'Waterford Electronics *is* facing some pretty stiff competition these days. The last thing a company needs is to have cash-flow problems in the middle of a crisis. It will soon become necessary to make several adjustments to the way the firm operates.'

She glanced at him warily. 'What sort of adjustments?'

'Nothing too dramatic. Just a bit of streamlining. A little more push in the sales department. A little more care about company spending.'

'This is beginning to have a familiar ring,' she said grimly.

'Don't put that delicious frown on your face,' he smiled. 'I'm not telling you to cut all your firm's philanthropic expenses. I'm just suggesting that there are ways of giving profits back to the community without putting the company's resources at risk. Your competitors,' he added meaningfully, 'are not throwing *their* money away on grants, bursaries and sports facilities.'

'That's why we're different,' she retorted. 'Because we care about the future of this town. Because we care about the families who work for us!'

'Granted,' Damian said. 'But there's no reason why Waterford Electronics shouldn't become more profitable, without sacrificing the benevolent work it does. Braithwaite and Denison take the simple-minded view that just cutting out the charity marathons and selling off the land is going to make them rich men. It's not as easy as that.'

'Tell me what the solution is, then,' Kirby invited. 'You said I wouldn't like it. But I'm willing to consider anything . . . within reason.'

'I'm still pulling the details together,' he replied. 'I'll give you the full plan in a few days' time.'

'You got me up here on false pretences!' she accused. 'You said you'd tell me what the plan was this afternoon.'

He considered her thoughtfully. In this light the blue in his eyes was dominated by the grey, giving his stare a brooding quality that seemed to reach deep inside her. 'Now is not the moment,' he said flatly. 'But I can tell you this much. The solution to your problem lies in two courses of action. One is to make Waterford Electronics as competitive as possible, which will silence your critics, and get them on your side, if that can be done. The other is to round up all the shares that are now in hands other than yours, Sir Malcolm Denison's, or Roderick Braithwaite's. To make sure that as much of the voting stock as possible is concentrated in one place, so that you cannot be challenged again.'

'That's easier said than done,' Kirby said with a sigh. 'I told you, Damian, I'm only a rich woman on paper. Keith left me all his shares in the company—but I can't sell them. I don't have any cash, just an income from Waterford Electronics. I certainly don't have anything like the money to go around buying up all the shares other shareholders might have.'

'There are problems,' he conceded. 'That's why I need a few more days to get the finer points tied up.'

Her face fell. 'Ah, well. It sounded too good to be true.'

'Trust me,' he laughed. 'And don't be such a pessimist.'

Kirby shrugged, not bothering to hide her disappointment. It was all very well to theorise about such things; putting them into practice was a different prospect altogether. 'Thanks for trying, anyway.'

'Let's have a rest before we go back,' he suggested.
She agreed readily. Between the morning's exercise and
the champagne she was now feeling rather sleepy, and
a doze would be welcome before the long ride back to
Braythorpe.

She cleared up the remains of their meal, leaving the
chicken scraps under a bush where the badgers and foxes
would find them. In the meantime, Damian had folded
the blankets into a makeshift bed. She eyed him askance.
He grinned.

'It's too cold for a proper assault on your virtue, my
love. But I *am* offering my manly shoulder as a pillow
for your fair head.'

'No funny stuff?' she challenged.

'No funny stuff,' he promised. 'Come.'

His arms did seem a great deal more welcoming a
cushion than the stony ground, but it was with a great
many misgivings that Kirby curled up beside him, and
let him slide a strong arm under her shoulders.

However, as soon as she laid her head on his chest a
delicious languor stole through her whole body, and she
felt herself relaxing with the guilelessness of a child. And,
before she even had time to even contemplate the wisdom
of what she was doing, she was asleep.

She awoke to the patter of drops in the trees overhead.
A couple of hours had passed. The threatening sky had
begun to weep at last, and, though they were sheltered
where they lay, she could smell the rain in the air.

She lay as she had fallen asleep, snuggled close up to
Damian, his arms linked defensively around her. So intimate, she thought dreamily. So warm and wonderful,
to lie like this, cradled against his strong man's body.
She could hear his deep, regular breathing, could smell

the clean smell of his hair, that fragrance which stirred her senses more strongly than any cognac.

It was a long time since she'd lain in a man's arms like this. A long time. Not since Keith's death. And that had been very different from this.

The way Damian held her was so protective. So possessive. Even in sleep he seemed to be watching over her, guarding her. She'd never had this sense of security before. Nor this sense of...what was it? Something new, yet so achingly familiar. Something she knew so well from dreams, and yet had never felt in waking.

It would be so easy to call it love. So dreadfully easy to let that dam wall crumble, and feel the weight of the water spilling out, tumbling down the rocks, exploding into a force that could not be controlled, could not be contained...

One hand was clasped around her shoulder. Strong hands, precise and yet sensual. Hands whose touch on her body could make a fever rage. She battled that memory down, unable to deal with it right now.

She moved her head gently so that she could see his face. He was so beautiful. In sleep he looked younger, not so commanding. His lashes were thick and dark enough to be the envy of any woman. The curving laughter-lines on either side of his mouth were relaxed.

How in God's name had she been so foolish as to let him back into her life? Beguiled by his promise that he could slay her dragons. But it had been more than that. Much more.

From the moment she'd set eyes on him at Caroline's house she'd known that she was treading the edge of the precipice again.

If she'd had Keith beside her, she'd have been able to draw back and save herself. But without Keith she had been wandering along that crumbling edge, with the whirlpool waters swirling down below, waiting to claim her soul.

She reached up with infinite delicacy, and touched the deeply carved line of his mouth with her fingertips. His lips were velvet-soft, warm. She recalled their kiss with a painful stab of desire. When perdition was so enchantingly sweet, should she bother about saving her soul? Why not just let herself go, let the current drag her down, down, down?

She felt him stir slightly, and drew her hand guiltily away.

'Don't stop,' Damian said softly. 'I was enjoying that.'

'Sorry,' she said in embarrassment. 'Did I wake you?'

'No. The rain did. I was just lying here thinking about what it felt like to have you in my arms.'

'You've probably got pins and needles in every limb,' she said with remorse. 'I've treated you like a mattress for about two hours.'

'I'm tingling,' he agreed. 'But not because you've cut my circulation off. Actually, my problem is quite the reverse.'

He drew her close to him with powerful arms, and pressed his mouth deep into the chestnut curls of her hair. She felt him inhale her scent deep into his lungs.

'God, you smell so marvellous,' he rumbled.

'I'm not wearing any perfume,' she replied unsteadily.

'Yes, you are. You smell of the moors. Of heather and rain and a beautiful woman's silky skin...' She closed her eyes helplessly as she felt his lips touch her temple. He kissed her there, then again and again, braiding a daisy-chain of kisses that stole down the curve of her cheek to the corner of her mouth, where the skin became soft and agonisingly sensitive.

'Damian, you promised,' she whispered, terrified by the hot rush of excitement that he was sending through her veins. She turned her head aside to avoid the sweet torment of his mouth.

But he drew her face gently back to his. The wonderful, deep eyes gazed into hers, drowning her in their depths. 'Are my kisses so unwelcome?' he murmured.

'They're an unnecessary complication.' Her tongue tripped clumsily over the words, betraying how disturbed she was.

'There's nothing complicated about a kiss.'

'Depends who's giving it. Who's receiving it.'

'I'm giving,' he whispered, 'you're receiving...' He kissed her full on the lips, his mouth covering hers with a decisive passion that overwhelmed her defences—such as they had been.

She tried not to respond, clenching her teeth and making fists out of her hands. But the intoxicating pressure of his kiss melted her strength, making her jaw relax, opening the moist intimacy of her mouth to his invasion.

She had not been kissed like this since she was eighteen years old. Not since that night in the summer-house. But there was nothing adolescent about this kiss. It was devastatingly adult, an erotic caress that was almost shocking in what it did to her. She felt his tongue search for her own, slippery and firm in contrast to her own meltingly timid response. The heat in her veins was rising, her pulses starting to pound like pagan drums.

She found herself clinging to him, as if to a rock in a raging sea. His hand slid under the protection of her jacket, under the layers of wool and cotton she wore beneath, until his palm claimed the silky skin of her flanks. She arched to him unrestrainedly, tacitly begging his tongue to probe deeper, to satisfy her mounting hunger for him.

She felt his hand caress her skin, sliding upwards to claim the firm curves of her breasts. Her nipples thrust against his fingertips, hardening unbearably under the expert, tantalising caress.

It was as though her body had been a dead tree that had suddenly covered itself in blossom. Suddenly, the erotic centres of her body were aching with need, aching with a hunger she'd never known before. As he touched the exquisite peaks of her nipples, she could feel her own thighs moving in unmistakable invitation, her loins molten and ready for love.

Now every touch of her clothes against her own aroused body was a torment. She wanted to undress, here under this lowering sky, with the thunder of Sovereign Force in the air, and give herself to Damian. Give herself with the abandon of a sacrifice on a barbarian altar...

As her thigh pressed between his, she encountered the thrusting pressure of his desire, and heard the deep rumble of his response, like the purring of a panther.

Kirby's hand slid down his hard, flat belly, feeling the robust musculature beneath her palm...until her fingertips reached him, traced the column of his erect manhood. She felt his body shudder with the shocking pleasure her touch gave him, and a wild exultation filled her heart at the realisation that she could affect him just as intensely as he affected her.

Her fingers grew bolder, exploring, caressing, until he gave a rough gasp, and reached down to catch her wrist in his fingers. For a blazing moment, he pressed her palm even more fiercely against the outline of his manhood. Then he drew her away, his breathing ragged and uneven.

He looked down at her with eyes that were the stormy colour of the North Sea. There was a deeper flush on his high cheekbones. 'This isn't the time, Kirby,' he said harshly. 'And it isn't the place.'

'It's too late to stop now!'

'Almost,' he growled. 'But I still have a shred of sanity left.'

'Damn you,' she whispered. 'What are you doing to me?'

'Nothing that you haven't done to me,' he replied. 'How have we managed to stay apart for so long, Kirby? We need each other so much!'

'You were the one who left!' She touched his cheek with trembling fingers. 'You were the one who broke us apart!'

'So you rushed off and married Keith Waterford.'

'I didn't *rush off*,' she flung back at him. 'Keith threw me a lifebelt. I was in no position to refuse. Damian, you said you didn't want me round you any more!'

'Don't,' he said, shutting his eyes. 'You don't know how many times I've heard myself say those words...and cursed myself. If only you knew, Kirby. If only you had the faintest notion——' He clamped his mouth shut, biting off the words. He kissed her instead, with hard passion. 'Come on,' he commanded. 'Let's go before it really *is* too late.'

It took a feat of will to rise on her shaking legs, and brush the twigs of heather from her disordered clothes. This sick pang of desire inside her—how long had it been since she'd felt it? Had Keith, gentle, sweet man that he had been, ever made her feel remotely like this?

She knew the answer. Only Damian had the power to make love to her in a kiss, to ravish her soul with a touch.

His big, powerful body moved with effortless grace as he organised the horses, and helped her up into the saddle. Kirby looked out across the rainy moors, feeling the unyielding leather of the saddle press against the secret arousal in her loins. It was a pressure that only intensified the ache, the dragging pain of unfulfilment. She almost would rather have walked all the way back than face the ride—if her legs hadn't been so pathetically weak.

'We're going to get soaked,' Damian said, mounting his own horse. 'This wasn't the best day to choose for an...escapade.'

'I'll never forget it,' she told him quietly. She had spoken so softly that she wasn't sure he had heard her above the rain-permeated wind. But then the smoky eyes met hers, and she caught the glint of his wonderful smile.

'Neither will I,' he said. He held her gaze for a moment longer until she felt the lurching of her heart as his unspoken thoughts touched her.

Then he nudged his horse into motion, and they set off through the fine drizzle back down into the dale. She pulled the hood of her jacket up over her hair, and squinted against the wind. There was no sign of the rain letting up. It was going to be a wet ride. But nothing mattered, not compared to the wild singing in her heart.

And for a long, long time, as her horse picked his careful way through the purple swaths of moorland heather, she could still hear the glorious thunder of the waterfall in her ears.

CHAPTER SEVEN

As DAMIAN had predicted, they were both soaked to the bone by the time they reached the stables where they'd hired the horses. The wind had blown the rain into every possible gap in their clothing, and even Kirby's hood hadn't saved her hair from turning into a dishevelled mass of dripping curls.

They surveyed one another ruefully. 'A very romantic but wet afternoon,' was Damian's judgement. 'I think a cold whisky and a hot bath are in order.'

She knew he was staying at the Beechings, a private hotel outside Braythorpe. Elegant as it was, it would not offer the comforts of home, and she heard herself offering hesitantly, 'I've got both at my place... if you want to come back with me?'

'Yes,' he said firmly. 'I definitely want to come back with you, Kirby.'

He spread a rug over the seats of his Porsche. 'They'll still get soaked,' she mourned over the beautiful leather upholstery.

'Things are meant to be used,' he replied. 'Don't fuss.'

It was raining even harder as they pulled up outside the Lodge, and darkness was setting in. Any delays in their descent from Sovereign Force, she reflected, and they might have ended up spending the night out on the moors. 'Which first?' she asked him. 'Hot water or cold whisky?'

'Hot water,' he decided.

She led Damian to an upstairs bedroom, and showed him the bathroom. With its gleaming brass taps and marble fittings, it was an opulent relic from a bygone age, and he gazed round admiringly. 'Another period piece. I'll say one thing for the Victorians—they knew what comfort was all about.'

'And there's plenty of hot water,' she smiled, turning on the taps. 'Towels are over there...and I'll see if I can find you something dry to wear.'

'Something of Keith's?' he asked, meeting her eyes.

She shook her head. 'I gave all his clothes to Oxfam. But I've got some over-sized jumpers that might fit you, and I might even find a pair of jeans somewhere. I'll put your wet clothes in the tumble-drier in the meantime so, at worst, you might have to sit around in this for an hour or two.'

'Thank you, dear,' he said solemnly, taking the dressing-gown she passed him.

'It's mine,' she told him, 'but it's huge. It ought to fit you.'

He hauled off his sodden jersey in one fluid movement. She couldn't stop her eyes from glancing at his body. He was magnificently built. There was so little fat on his frame that she could see the hard muscles under his skin as he moved. The tan he'd picked up in Portugal was already starting to fade, but his skin had an almost Mediterranean darkness next to her own. Dark hair etched its way down his muscular chest, covering his flat belly in a disturbingly animal pelt.

He smiled at her, his eyes sultry. 'Playing house is quite fun, isn't it?'

'Depends who you're playing with,' she replied, trying to sound normal.

'It might be pleasant to play with you,' he purred.

'Wendy Catchpole has already marked your card,' she retorted. 'Go play with her.'

'Witch,' he grinned.

Steam was starting to fill the bathroom, chastely cloaking his near-nudity. But even so, as he began to unbuckle his denims, she turned and fled.

She went down to put his wet clothes in the tumble-drier. The big house was silent—it was the staff's afternoon off—but for once it did not echo around her. Damian's presence seemed to warm the whole place, his aura chasing out the loneliness that was so often her only companion here. She left the machine spinning, and went up to her bedroom. There she hunted out the biggest jerseys she could find while her own bath ran, coming up with a weird and wonderful assortment of things. She left them in his bedroom.

Soaking in the bathtub, she thought over the day, looking absently down at her own naked body. She had never been voluptuous, but that had never particularly worried her. Too many curves on a petite figure often resulted in dumpiness. And, whatever else she was, she was not dumpy. Her figure was delicate, the flare of her hips as graceful as a classical Greek vase. Her breasts were high and firm, their tips peaked with rosebud nipples. She had excellent legs, with slim, firm thighs. Where they met, a delicately shaded triangle of curls shimmered in the water.

I know your body so well, he had said. I've thought of it so many times over the past six years. Remembering its sweetness, its delicacy.

Pretty words. Did he know how much they affected her? Why had he hinted at deeper feelings, feelings much more serious than friendship or old times' sake?

Why had he been coming on so strong? This afternoon, up there at Sovereign Force, he could not have been more loving. Dreamily, she watched her own nipples tighten at the erotic memory. If he'd wanted to make her desire him even more than she already did, he had certainly succeeded. There was still an ache in her stomach where arousal had blazed.

But suspicion nagged at her like a ghost. For a man who was going to be married, 'Some time in the new year, when the pressure of work drops a little,' he was showing a remarkable amount of interest in a woman who was really no more than a memory from his past.

Was he leading her to destruction, all over again? Was there some cruel force in him that wanted to make her love him, and then rip her heart into pieces?

She felt sick at the thought. No. No man could be so cruel. It just wasn't possible. If she'd really thought it was, she'd have run, run as far and as fast as her legs would carry her...

She soaped herself, rinsing away her doubts with the day's residue. The question of Damian's sincerity didn't arise, because she had no intention whatsoever of falling for him again. She might be in love with him—she might stay in love with him until she was an old, old lady—but that didn't mean she had to give him her soul.

No, she would stay in touch with him until he had found a solution to her problems with the company. She had her doubts about that. From what he'd said this afternoon, his ideas were revolving around spending sums of money that she didn't remotely have. Still, he was the most intelligent man she knew, and if he couldn't come up with an answer, then no one could. And already his very shadow had sent Sir Malcolm Denison and Roderick Braithwaite scuttling for cover.

She'd be a fool to reject his help. Caroline had been right—in this hard world women needed all the help they could get. Perhaps she should be more like Caroline... and deliberately use her femininity to keep protective males around her.

The trouble was, Damian Holt was not so much a protective male as a big, hungry panther, licking his lips in her direction.

When she'd finished her bath, she washed and dried her hair, and got into a fluffy sweater and velvet cord trousers, and went to see if Damian had finished his bath yet. He had, and was wearing the gown she had given him. It was big enough to cover him, but his muscular chest and throat were bare, and his dark hair was sleeked back from his temples.

'Aren't any of the clothes big enough?' she asked. 'I thought some of the jerseys might fit.'

'Which?' he smiled. 'The pink cashmere or the yellow roses? At least this covers my modesty without compromising my macho image. Besides, I like this. It smells of you.'

She didn't reply to that. 'Are you hungry?'

'No. But I'm ready to go down for that whisky now.'

'We don't have to go downstairs. There's a fire in my parlour.'

' "Said the spider to the fly",' he murmured.

'You're quite safe from me, Damian,' she assured him drily.

'I didn't feel so safe this afternoon,' he pointed out.

She flushed at the memory, and turned. 'Well, you're out of danger now, I assure you.' She led him to the upstairs sitting-room which she called 'her parlour'.

It was actually a television-room, with deep, comfortable settees, its walls lined with well-stocked bookshelves. Mrs Carstairs, as always, had made sure there was a fire burning brightly in the grate, and the velvet curtains had been drawn against the rainy, misty night.

Damian looked around, his eyes taking in the telling details of the room—piles of magazines, a half-finished novel, a pile of embroidery, a box of her favourite bitter chocolates. 'This is where you spend your evenings,' he guessed.

'Yes,' she said, inclining her head.

'Sitting here, all alone, with your chocolates and your book and your television.'

'You make it sound very gloomy,' she said with a faint smile. 'I spend some of my most contented hours up here, Damian. My life is a very peaceful, quiet one these days.'

'Your life shouldn't be peaceful and quiet,' he said gently. 'You're too special a person. You should be among things that fill you with joy. Not sitting in the silence, alone.'

'Everybody tells me I'm special,' she shrugged. 'All I want is peace and quiet. When your life's been hit by tragedy, it doesn't exactly leave you hankering for the bright lights. You need time to heal. I'll get you that drink.'

Damian's eyes followed her as she went to the cabinet, and poured him the whisky he had asked for. She brought it over to him, and they sank down into the embrace of the deep-cushioned settee. 'Your retreat is certainly comfortable,' he conceded, stretching out his long legs. He noticed her empty hands. 'Not having anything?'

'I don't usually drink spirits. I only had the whisky the other night to give me courage.'

'Did you need courage?'

'To face you, yes, I did.'

'Do I scare you that much?'

She curled her legs under her, and contemplated him, her chin cupped in her hand. 'Do you have any idea how much you hurt me, Damian?' she asked quietly.

He winced. 'Tell me.'

'Perhaps you thought I was still a child. But an eighteen-year-old woman is very much an adult. With an adult's capacity to love. And an adult's capacity to have her heart broken. I don't blame you for making me love you. You couldn't help that. But what you did to me that night, the way you rejected me...' She shrugged painfully. 'These things leave a scar. The place is still tender. When you're around, I tend to walk on eggshells.'

He stared down into his whisky, swirling the amber liquid slowly round and round. Then he drained the glass at a gulp, as though it were bitter medicine. 'Yes,' he said in a curt voice. 'I *did* think you were a child, Kirby. It took me a long time to realise that you weren't—that you had become a woman, and I was just refusing to see it. And by then you had married Keith.' He looked up at Kirby, his eyes dark pools. 'I'm ten years older than you. I watched you grow up. And I always loved you, whatever you may think.'

'As a brother?' she asked, her mouth dry.

'I loved you,' he said simply. 'And I was far from blind to the way you felt about me. While you were still a girl, even when you were an adolescent, the adoration in your eyes filled me with joy. Then I began to worry.'

'What about?'

'That our relationship was no longer good for you. That it was just the opposite, in fact—a crippling infatuation with a much older man, something that would stop you from reaching emotional maturity.'

'I don't understand what you're saying, Damian.'

'During your teens I would look at you. I would see a girl who had never so much as kissed another boy. You would hardly go out with boys of your own age. You only had eyes for me... and I was a grown man in my twenties. And I would see the concern in your parents' eyes. I knew what they were thinking. That my presence in your life was too strong for your own good. They were right. Then you suddenly became not only charming and sweet, but also beautiful. You were suddenly a sexual adult, with a woman's figure and a woman's eyes. I just couldn't believe that you had a woman's mind to match.'

'I did,' she whispered.

'I didn't believe it,' he repeated. 'You were seventeen, going on eighteen. I was already almost twenty-eight. I knew that business was inevitably taking me to London. I knew that I would only have to ask, and you would have come with me. As my wife. I don't think that was vanity, just certainty.'

'I'd have come as your lover, Damian. As your slave.'

'*Slave,*' he repeated with a bitter expression. 'Yes. That's the word. You were enslaved. Whether to me— or just to an ideal of love, I had no way of telling. I only knew that you had never so much as looked at another man. You hadn't had a chance to! I'd been the dominant feature in your life ever since you'd worn pig-tails.' He paused, gathering his thoughts. 'It sounds,' he said wryly, 'as though I'm being very big-headed about all this. But I was trying to be just the reverse. I was desperate to be responsible about you. Desperate to do the right thing for you. Not necessarily to make you happy in the short term, but to give your life a chance to expand in the long term. I couldn't bear the thought that I hadn't allowed you to have all the opportunities you deserved.'

'The only opportunity I wanted was to be at your side,' she said. Her fingers were twisting restlessly together, her face pale and tense.

'I know. But I wanted more than that for you. That night in the summer-house——' He drew a deep breath. 'That night in the summer-house something happened that I'd been dreading for a long time. There was another side of my love for you, a side that had grown with your growing womanhood. I wanted you, Kirby. I wanted you desperately badly. It didn't matter how many other women I had around me...yours was the only face I saw. Yours was the only body that I desired. I tried so hard to suppress that. I was terrified of what would happen if I ever let it control me. Once we'd become lovers there would no longer have been any logic, any responsibility. And on your eighteenth birthday, the night I wanted you to be so happy, that side of my love suddenly dominated me.'

Kirby's heart was pounding like a hammer, flooding her breast with pain. It was hard for her to breathe. 'Then...you *did* want me?'

'I wanted you more than I believed possible. I remember how it started. In the garden. You were babbling some nonsense.' His eyes were on hers, but they were looking far into the past the two of them shared. 'You started crying. I took your face in my hands, meaning to say something flippant, to cheer you up. But instead I was kissing you...kissing your lips...' He closed his eyes for a moment, his voice growing harsh and tortured. 'I'd never felt anything like it before. It was so powerful that it frightened me. It seemed to be dragging me where I didn't want to go, like——'

'Like a whirlpool,' she whispered.

'Yes,' he nodded, opening his eyes. 'That's what it was like. My body was trembling. I was saying words that I'd rather have bitten my tongue off than utter. We'd kissed so many times in our lives, but never like that. I desired you so much, Kirby. I was barely in control of myself. And when I finally realised what I was doing I was devastated. Incredulous that I could have been such a fool, so weak! I reacted with fury, Kirby.'

'I know how you reacted,' she said sickly.

They were silent for a long while, Kirby sorrowfully reliving the terrible pain of that night. At last, Damian spoke again. 'The next day, of course, I could have come to you and apologised. But I knew that if I tried to explain I'd only end up in the same—what was your word?—the same whirlpool. Our relationship had changed for ever. It was time for me to go. Though I knew I'd hurt us both in the cruellest way, it seemed to me to be the best solution. A way of tearing us apart, so that you could follow your own destiny, and I mine. I told myself that I would give you time, time to grow up and learn your own mind. And one day, I promised myself, I'd come back to find you. But, when I did, Kirby Bryant was gone. I found only Mrs Keith Waterford, another man's wife.'

Kirby got up abruptly. 'I think I will have that whisky,' she said.

'You can give me a refill,' he agreed wryly, passing her his glass. Her hands were unsteady as she poured the drinks. She came back to sit beside him on the settee.

Damian raised his glass to her with a half-smile. 'If it's any consolation, Kirby, you're still the most desirable woman I've ever known.'

His words, and the soft tone with which they were uttered, made her flush. 'I suppose that's a compliment of a sort,' she muttered.

'Of a sort,' he agreed, amused.

She sipped the drink, making a face at the taste. 'Well,' she said with irony, 'it's always nice to know your heart was broken for your own good.'

'Has anyone told you that you have a rather vinegary sense of humour?' he smiled. 'I suffered too, Kirby. No less than you did. Looking back, I still somehow feel I did the right thing. Had we made love that night in the summer-house, we'd almost certainly have got married. And if we'd married then, with you still not out of your teens, we'd probably have been divorced by now, and miserable as hell. As it is, we've learned to appreciate each other.'

'Speak for yourself,' she said, raising her eyebrows in a school-marmish way.

'All right. I've learned to appreciate *you*.' He reached out to touch her soft, clean hair. 'I can't ask for forgiveness, Kirby,' he said gently. 'I only ask for understanding. And pray that out of understanding comes...something more.'

'Oh, Damian,' she said unsteadily. 'Don't play any more games with me. I couldn't stand it.'

'I'm not playing games any more,' he insisted, his fingertips brushing her throat. 'You were right when you said it was never a game. Not even six years ago.'

'You made me care for you once before. Now you're back in my life, in very different circumstances. You're engaged to another woman, and you say things to me that make me feel...'

'Make you feel what?' he whispered.

She couldn't answer. He reached for her, and she melted into his arms with a little whimper. He drew her close, his mouth covering hers with tender possession, his hands sliding under her sweater to stroke the smooth skin of her back, her taut flanks, the satin ripples of her ribcage.

She whispered his name as he cupped her breasts, holding them in his palms, his thumbs slowly circling the peaks until they stood out in a taut entreaty for attention. He massaged the soft curves gently, the pleasure intensifying until she arched against him, passion flowing in her like a river.

Their embrace grew abandoned. If there had been a sense of restraint before, of doubt, there was none tonight. Kirby clung to Damian's strong shoulders, her lips seeking his with blind passion. She could feel the hard muscles of his body against her, was hotly aware of his nakedness under the gown. This time, she knew instinctively, there would be no hesitation at the brink. No second thoughts to tear them apart.

This time the maelstrom was going to pull them both into its whirling centre, and there would be no evasion.

Her heart was racing as she responded to Damian's kiss. Her hands cupped his face, slid down his throat, moving under the gown to claim the sinewy breadth of his shoulders, and caress the crisp, dark hair on his chest. He was all living muscle, taut and virile, his warm flesh unbelievably exciting under her touch.

She brushed his nipples with her palms, feeling their hard points erect with desire, just as her own were. Then she caressed his broad ribcage, her hands tapering down to his lean waist, pulling his gown aside to reveal his naked, muscled stomach.

'Kirby,' he said raggedly. 'I've wanted you so much today. I couldn't keep my eyes off you. There's never been any other woman for me...you know that, don't you?'

Her throat was tight, stopping her from uttering the foolish words that tomorrow she would have regretted. But right now she had never been so prepared for love, had never needed fulfilment with such a wild hunger.

To answer him, she leaned forward, and kissed his nipples, touching the dark points with her tongue so that he groaned, deep in his chest. She could feel the potent arousal at his loins. It seemed so natural, so inevitable, that she would slide downwards, her hands preparing the way so that she could press her lips to the searing thrust of his manhood.

His body arched at the shocking eroticism of her caress. Yes, she thought with wild exultation, he had been right. She was no longer a virgin. No longer a girl, innocent and inexperienced. She was a mature, aware woman now, and able to meet him on a woman's terms.

Her mouth seemed to melt around him, drawing his arousal to a fierce abundance. She felt his spine arch like a bow, felt his almost tormented response to what she was able to make him feel. Passion was a pagan altar, surrounded by flames. She worshipped with unashamed delight, until Damian's fingers knotted in her hair, and drew her away. He did not speak. But one look at his face told her what she had done to him.

He was hers, she exulted. Hers, completely and without reservation. Whatever happened in the cold light of tomorrow, tonight Damian belonged to her.

He stretched out among the cushions, drawing her down on to him. In the silence, the fire crackled peacefully, its warmth touching their skins. Their mouths met as their bodies pressed together, thighs entwining, hands caressing each other's fevered skin. He pulled her jersey gently up over her head, exposing her naked torso. She shook her curly hair free, and smiled down at him. He smiled back into her eyes, so majestic, so beautiful.

'My, my,' he whispered, tracing the aphrodisiac buds of her nipples, 'haven't you grown up, Kirby Bryant...?'

'And you, Damian Holt...' wickedly, she touched both hands to his manhood, appraising the taut strength with which it rose from his loins to her '...you've grown, too.'

His eyes were dark with passion. 'It was worth waiting,' he said softly, 'to see you like this, so beautiful, so free. Worth every miserable, lonely moment.'

He unfastened her cord trousers with sure fingers, tugging them unhurriedly down over her hips. And then they were both unashamedly naked, embracing with gasping tenderness as their skin seemed to fuse. He rose over her, kissing her with an intensity that seemed to make her bones melt, robbing her of strength.

This time it was her turn to knot her fingers in his hair as he brushed her breasts with his mouth, his breath warm against the aroused, delicate skin. She felt his tongue trace the shape of her nipples, felt the hunger of his teeth, almost painful, as he claimed the rosy flesh.

Her need for him was like the thunder of the waterfall in her ears. She revelled in the pleasure of feeling him worship her body, as she had worshipped his, knowing that there would never be another man in her life. There never had been another man. He was everything to her, everything in the world...

His name drifted through her mind like a poem as his kisses covered her stomach, the smooth curve of her abdomen, reaching the intolerably sensitive skin of her thighs.

The emotion she'd felt so far had been only a teasing prelude to what she experienced now. She could not withstand Damian's gentle insistence that she open herself to him. Her thighs relaxed, and his mouth had free rein to roam where it pleased, its sensual caress discovering all her secrets, discovering an intensity of sexual pleasure that Kirby had never known.

There could be no inhibitions between them any more. As his tongue explored the melting centre of her need, tracing the electric pathways of pleasure that her body had never even known were there, she felt a sense of unity with him that transfigured everything else. The past, the future—none of the former or possible pains mattered any more. Only this mattered—this searing present, this current between them that was dragging her relentlessly to the brink, dragging her to the dangerous precipice of fulfilment——

As he had done a moment earlier, she was now compelled to arch away before it was too late, entreating him to have mercy.

He rose to take her in his arms, looking down at the flushed oval of her face with infinite adoration.

'I knew we would make love one day,' he said, caressing the chestnut curls away from her face. 'I've dreamed of it so many times, my love. In so many ways. And now my dream is alive, and in my arms——' he bent to kiss her yielding mouth '—and so very, very beautiful.'

She could only whisper his name as their bodies merged again, hands and lips mingling in the continuing arabesque of their passion. He was a lover with a passion she could only have imagined. With Keith, lovemaking had been kind, painless. But it had never approached the heights that Damian made her reach, teaching her to float in a new world, a new universe.

He adored her with his whole body, treating her with overwhelming strength, and yet with a petal-soft delicacy, seeming to know the sensitive curves and hollows of her body better than she knew them herself.

She had not known there were so many ways of being in love. She had not known there were so many ways to feel ecstasy. Finally she could bear it no longer, and dug her nails fiercely into his shoulders.

'No more,' she commanded with husky imperiousness. 'Make love to me, Damian. Now.'

'I've been waiting to hear you say that for a long time,' he whispered, moving over her. He took her in his arms, his mouth covering hers. Without clumsiness, without haste, his body found the entrance to her own.

And then he was entering her, and Kirby felt that fulfilment she had always known was there, and had never encountered before. A fulfilment so intense it was almost like pain, almost like losing her virginity all over again.

She was liquid, drawing him in, so that he filled her utterly, sliding deep into his place within her body, until she felt him with every element of her womanhood, with her womb, with her soul.

Kirby clung to him in abandon. At first his love-making was so gentle and slow that she moaned her frustration, until the power and intensity grew, a rhythmical, swelling movement that flooded her senses, so that pleasure was no longer just there, where their bodies joined, but everywhere, in every physical and spiritual inch of her.

Nothing so intense could be prolonged for long. She did not want it to be prolonged, did not want artifice to come between them. Later, they would learn how to make this heaven last, make it fill whole nights and days.

Right now, she craved union with him, consummation for what they had both wanted for so long. The movement of her body told him that without words, and he thrust into her with deliberate, irresistible skill, urging them both to the very edge, over the edge, into the thunder...

She had an almost visionary memory of Sovereign Force, of the long, hurtling fall of all that vast weight of white water, dashing off the rocks, exploding into spray that danced with rainbows.

And then she knew what the whirlpool was—the whirlpool that had haunted her half her life. It had her in its arms, spinning her as if she were a leaf, drawing her into the chaotic centre of its power.

But not with pain or fear. Instead, the power was a joy she'd never reached before, a bright force that she did not want to resist, even if she could have resisted. And beneath the swirling waters was not cold darkness, but dazzling light, heat, the energy of life itself, that was exploding from his body into hers.

She did not know she was crying until Damian kissed the tears away from her wet lashes, whispering her name. He was still erect inside her, and he remained there as he kept kissing her, caressing her face, whispering endearments, as though he could not get enough of her, and no act of love could satisfy his desire for her.

'Damian,' she choked, 'my darling...'

'Was I too rough?' he whispered. 'I tried to hold back, but...' ,

'You were——' Like a storm. Like a miracle. She couldn't find the words, so she just closed her soaked lashes and held him tight.

In this exquisite afterglow, it was an added bliss to feel him still within her body, still filling her soul with his heat. It prolonged the pleasure endlessly, kept the sweet ache alive.

And as she felt him move again, she gasped, 'Don't you ever get enough?'

'Not of you,' he whispered. 'Never enough of you, my love.'

She arched on the peak of sensation. It was too soon to start again, too soon to plunge back into that engulfing whirlpool!

But her voice rustled in her throat, saying otherwise. And, as the throbbing rhythm began again, it was no longer too soon. It was time, now, and again...and again...

* * *

She was awakened by his kiss, centuries later.

She surfaced from the warm depths of her sleep, clinging to him under the covers. 'Damian?'

'I'm sorry to wake you,' he whispered. 'But I have to go. And I couldn't bear to leave without saying goodbye.'

She was still dazed, and she opened her eyes in troubled confusion. Her tender nipples brushed cotton. They were in her bedroom, lying together in her bed. How had they got there?

Then she remembered. Remembered him carrying her, naked and dreamy with love, in his arms. He had laid her on her own bed. And there he had taken her again, his passion inexhaustible, as drivingly urgent as that very first time, even though she'd lost count of the times they'd loved one another during this glorious night.

'Don't go,' she pleaded, her mouth seeking his.

'It's six-thirty in the morning,' he said, stroking her face. 'Your staff will be arriving soon. And you can imagine how quickly gossip will spread if they find me here. I don't want you to suffer that, Kirby. I have to go.'

'When will I see you?' she begged.

'At lunchtime. Meet me at L'Escargot at one-thirty.'

'I'll be there, my love.'

'Go back to sleep now. You've earned it.'

'Your clothes are still in the drier.'

'Well, I hope your Mrs Carstairs doesn't decide to arrive early,' he smiled, 'or she's in for a shock.'

He slipped out of bed, and Kirby looked up at his magnificent, naked body. She reached out and caressed him with the intimate possession that only a lover was allowed. 'Damian,' she whispered, 'I've never experienced anything like that... not ever in my life.'

'Nor me,' he said. 'Don't remind me, Kirby. Or Braythorpe will never hear the end of it.'

'You're amazing,' she said, seeing what she had done to him. 'Don't you ever get tired?'

'I told you last night...' he bent and kissed her lips lingeringly '...not of you.'

Then he was gone.

She lay curled up in the warm place he had left, her whole being concentrated on her love for him. She wanted to keep it there, preserve it inside her, and never let it go. But a night of unaccustomed passion had exhausted her, and she drifted swiftly back into the warm depths...

CHAPTER EIGHT

As SHE got out of the Jaguar in the restaurant car park, Kirby felt all the radiance of a woman in love. It was a feeling that could hardly be explained, a sensation of being more beautiful, more alive, more feminine than she had ever been before. A feeling that champagne, and not blood, was running in her veins, that life was no longer grey and empty, but an adventure of limitless beautiful possibilities.

Even the weather had changed to echo her emotions. The rain of yesterday had cleared away in the night, and a brilliant cobalt sky arched overhead. It made a glorious backdrop to the rich autumn colours of the trees, whose red and gold leaves were barely stirring in the breeze. The sun was warm on her skin.

She had chosen her clothes with care this morning, and she knew that the amethyst shade of her silk suit was one of her best colours. She had set it off with a cream scarf, and she felt instinctively that, if she could ever lay claim to beauty, she had it now.

And there was another detail—one which she wondered rather uncomfortably whether Damian would notice: just before coming out, she had twisted the wedding-ring from the third finger of her left hand.

It had given her heart an agonising wrench to do so. She'd closed her eyes, and seen Keith's gentle smile. Remembered the day he had put it on, in the old church in Braythorpe's main square. Five years of marriage, cut short by a tragic motorway accident. Five years of her life, coming to an end. She'd felt the tears spill unchecked from her eyes, and slide hotly down her cheeks. She'd said a silent goodbye to her late husband, paying tribute to his goodness, his kindness, his humanity.

Then she'd taken a deep, shuddering breath, and had laid the braided gold band down on her dressing-table.

Drying her tears, she had told herself that Keith was gone. That he would not have wanted her to remain alone. That she was not being unfaithful to his memory. She would always remember him with love, and with respect. And, if she did nothing else in her life, she had long ago vowed that she would make sure Keith's company continued as he would have wanted it to. And she was going to carry that intention through.

But one phase of her life had ended now. And another was just beginning. She had no choice but to go on with her life.

Now, as she walked to the restaurant, she felt joy flood her at the prospect of seeing Damian again. Her heart was trembling with excitement.

Not that he had been away from her thoughts for a second of this beautiful day. If she needed no other reminder, the intimate throbbing of her loins spoke of the rampant desire he had shown last night, the hunger that could not apparently be slaked. It was a sweetly tender memory of what he had done to her. Of how well he had loved her... better than she had ever been loved before.

She fought down the memories as she walked into the foyer of L'Escargot, to be welcomed by Maurice, the smiling *maître d'hôtel*. He kissed her hand as always, greeting her in French. She exchanged a few pleasantries in the same language as he led her into the restaurant.

'*Voilà,*' Maurice smiled, ushering her forward. '*Vos amis*, Madame Waterford.'

Damian rose from his chair, his handsome face wearing, most unusually for him, no expression at all. His eyes were dark and sombre. Kirby felt her own vulnerable smile fade in confusion as he extended a formal hand to greet her, instead of the tender kiss she had expected.

And then—how could she have been so blind? A woman's ridiculous emotion had put blinkers on her— she finally noticed Wendy Catchpole, seated at Damian's side.

The wide, rather cold green eyes met hers with a shock like iced water on warm skin.

'Hello, Kirby,' Damian said coolly. 'Wendy came back early from London. I thought she might as well come along to our little...business lunch.' His eyes were on hers all the time, and he was obviously picking his words with great care. 'I hope you don't mind?'

'I don't mind at all,' Kirby heard her own voice say, almost naturally. 'Hello, Wendy. Nice to see you back in Braythorpe.' She felt the momentary cool pressure of the other woman's fingers on her own. Then she sank down into her seat, just before her legs gave way.

Wendy tossed her long blonde hair back. 'Yes,' she said with her slightly metallic laugh, 'it seems I got back just in time. Darling Damian was nowhere to be found when I got to the hotel late last night. And he didn't come home until breakfast-time this morning, with some story about a reunion with old classmates. Highly suspicious, wouldn't you say, Kirby?'

Kirby felt a sick pain flood her stomach, filling her with nausea. 'Not necessarily,' she forced herself to reply, not meeting Damian's eyes. 'Your fiancé has lots of friends in this area. They probably sat drinking whisky until dawn.'

'I do hope you're right,' the blonde said. She laughed again, and stroked Damian's cheek with scarlet-nailed fingers. 'Not that I'm going to make a fuss, darling, am I? We agreed that we weren't going to be stupidly possessive about each other. Our marriage is going to be sophisticated and modern—like us.' She kissed his cheek, her lipsticked mouth almost touching Damian's. 'We don't let insignificant little details come between us. We keep our attention on the important things of life.'

'How nice,' Kirby said with an empty smile. She prayed that her face hadn't gone as white as it felt. She still could not bear to look at Damian.

This was unbearable.

She'd left all this behind her six years ago.

This bitter, bitter experience of sitting with Damian while another woman—a woman whose rights over him she would never have—stroked his cheek and flirted, and revelled in her possession. This wretched, silent misery compounded of jealousy, hopelessness, and that awful, crushing sense of inferiority.

If her legs had retained any strength, she'd have got up right then and walked out without a backward glance. But she knew that if she stood up now she would probably crumple, and make an utter, irreclaimable fool of herself. Damn him. *Damn* him.

'That's a very pretty colour,' Wendy commented with gracious condescension. 'It really quite suits you.'

'Thank you,' she replied in the same insincere tone as the compliment had been delivered. 'I like your jacket. It looks like Chanel?'

'It is Chanel,' Wendy said, touching the gold buttons. 'There's something different about you, Kirby...have you changed your hairstyle?'

'No,' she replied.

'There *is* a difference,' Wendy insisted.

Damian turned to the *maître d'hôtel*. '*Vous avez la carte, s'il vous plaît, Maurice?*'

'*Oui*, Monsieur Holt,' he beamed, snapping his fingers at one of the waiters to bring the menus over to their table. 'There are fresh oysters today, and the lobster is excellent. Enjoy your meal.'

'It's really too funny,' Wendy drawled as Maurice left. 'A pretentious restaurant like this, in a sleepy little backwater like Braythorpe. Oysters and lobsters! Whatever next?'

'Maurice used to work in the Savoy Grill,' Damian said mildly, opening the menus, and passing one to Kirby. 'So did the chef. You won't find the food pretentious.'

Wendy laughed. 'Did I step on your Yorkshire toes, darling? Of course! This place has a special significance for you two, doesn't it?' She glanced at Kirby. 'Damian's told me how you and he used to come here together in those dear, dead days, long ago. Well, I'll risk the oysters *and* the lobsters, if it will please you. Does that soothe your hurt pride?'

'I'll just have a steak and salad. Kirby?'

Her stomach was too knotted to even contemplate food. 'Grilled sole,' she said, without thought.

Damian ordered the meal, while Kirby toyed with the silver cutlery, keeping her gaze down. She could feel Wendy Catchpole's eyes constantly on her, studying her face, her clothes, her hands. It was not a kindly scrutiny. She was picking up some very unfriendly vibrations from the tall, classically attractive blonde. Did Wendy have a suspicion that something had happened between her and Damian? Or was she simply still irritated about her fall the other day?

The waiter left to relay their order to the kitchen.

Kirby compelled herself to look at Damian at last, keeping her expression as aloof as she could manage.

'Lunch is officially under way,' she said in a flat tone. 'Shall we get down to business—if it won't be too boring for Wendy, that is?'

'I'm never bored by talk about money,' Wendy replied. 'Damian's been giving a lot of thought to your little company. Haven't you, darling?'

'Yes, I have,' Damian said. His manner was urbane, as always. But she knew him well enough to sense the strain under the poised demeanour. How had he allowed this hateful situation to evolve? she wondered, cursing him bitterly. He could have warned her, at least...not just let her walk into a brick wall like this.

He began discussing the circumstances that Waterford Electronics was in, and she tried to force herself to be attentive. Shut away the pain, she commanded herself. Later is for emotion. Now is for being strong.

Last night might never have happened. A dream of passion. An experience that had left no trace other than the throbbing in her loins, which was now becoming a sharp pain.

In Damian's face, in Damian's voice, not the slightest trace remained of last night's consuming lover. He spoke in precise, even tones, as though they were no more than friends—friends with little in common other than a purely business interest.

Wendy suddenly cut in triumphantly. 'I *knew* there was something different about you!' she exclaimed. 'Look. She's taken off her wedding-ring.'

Kirby could not stop her eyes from meeting Damian's. If he saw the pain in hers, it was reflected by a darkening of his own eyes. She knew that flash of darkness, often the only sign of deep emotion that Damian ever gave. 'Has she?' he asked indifferently.

'I noticed it particularly because it was an unusual design—three colours of gold, braided together, wasn't it?'

'Yes,' Kirby said.

'I'm very observant,' Wendy laughed in satisfaction. The cold green eyes glittered. 'Well, well. How significant. Does this mean you're putting yourself back in the marriage market, Kirby?'

'It doesn't mean anything,' she replied tersely. 'Since I no longer have a husband, I just decided that a wedding-ring was an indulgence I wasn't entitled to any more.'

'Quite,' Wendy said, her cold smile in place. 'But it *is* a pretty obvious signal, isn't it? I mean to say—the merry widow, and all that.'

Their food arrived, saving what was, for Kirby at least, a very raw moment. They ate in silence for a while, Wendy dealing with her oysters in professional style, Kirby no more than picking at her sole.

Damian, too, seemed to have no appetite. Though he cut his steak into a great many pieces, she noticed that very few went into his mouth. She derived a bitter satisfaction from that, at least.

'Go on,' she invited him coolly. 'You were discussing the question of the voting stock.'

'Yes,' he agreed. 'As I said the other day, the voting stock is the key to achieving what you want. From the information you gave me, there are quite a lot of shares spread out among various board members—members other than Sir Malcolm and Roderick, that is—as well as in portfolios held by various local investors. It's vitally important to concentrate as many of those as possible in one place. That way, you have complete control of the direction Waterford Electronics goes in.'

'Agreed,' she shrugged. 'But, as I told you, Damian, that just isn't a feasible option. I don't have the cash to buy anyone else's shares.'

Wendy's metallic laugh rang out. 'You? Oh, *you* don't need cash, darling. Damian will see to all that.'

'I don't quite understand,' Kirby said stiffly.

'There's nothing to understand,' Wendy replied. 'The Holt Corporation are going to buy all the shares in your little company—including yours.'

Kirby turned to Damian in astonishment. 'What does she mean?' she demanded.

'Damian's buying you out,' Wendy cut in again, before Damian could speak. Her green eyes gleamed. 'Lock, stock and barrel, sweetie.'

'Is *that* your great plan?' Kirby gasped.

Damian glanced at Wendy, perhaps in irritation. 'I wouldn't have chosen to put it in the way Wendy's just done. But, in essence, I think that is the best solution to your problem.'

Kirby gaped at him in disbelief. 'So Roderick and Malcolm were right after all,' she said blankly. 'You *are* going for a buy-out!'

'I'm trying to find a way of keeping Waterford Electronics together,' he told her patiently. 'Consolidating control over the voting stock, so there can be no serious challenge from any single board member.'

'Consolidating?' Kirby's astonishment was fast turning into anger. 'Taking them all into your own hands, you mean. Well, the answer is no!'

'You haven't heard me out yet, Kirby.'

'I don't think I have to!' She pushed her plate away from her brusquely. 'There's no question of your getting my shares!'

'Let me finish,' he said evenly, his slate-blue eyes holding hers. 'I'm proposing to reorganise the structure

of the company. First of all, we would locate as many
shares as are available. They, and your own shares—the
ones Keith left you—would be bought up by the Holt
Corporation.'

'Of course,' she said tersely. 'Go on.'

'All the shares would pass into the control of a steering
company, which would now assume management of
Waterford Electronics. The steering company, of course,
would be a subsidiary of the Holt Corporation.
Waterford Electronics would now have the benefit of
our considerable expertise and experience—not to
mention a whole new range of customers and sources.
Incorporated in the working manifesto of that company
would be the principles that you want to preserve—the
donations to charity, the scholarships, the subsidies to
community centres—all the activities that Roderick
Braithwaite and Sir Malcolm Denison want to put a stop
to.'

'Except that you would now be the owner of Waterford
Electronics!'

'The steering company would be the owner.'

'The steering company which *you* would form, and
which would belong to the Holt Corporation!' Kirby was
so angry that her cheekbones were flushed, and her normally gentle brown eyes flashed fire. 'My God, Damian.
What kind of fool do you take me for?'

'I don't take you for a fool at all,' he replied. 'If you'll
let me finish, you'll see that this is a very good solution
to your problems.'

'So this has been your plan all along,' she said fiercely.
'While I thought you were putting together some way
of *helping* me, you were simply seeing a golden opportunity to line your own pockets!'

'You're wrong,' he told her quietly.

Wendy Catchpole had been watching Kirby's passionate outburst with unconcealed disdain. 'You're not being very grateful to darling Damian,' she said haughtily. 'He's been working very hard on your behalf. And it's no use saying no now. He's already spoken to several of your shareholders, and they've agreed to sell us their shares.'

Kirby gasped. 'You've already started buying up shares? Without even consulting me?'

'Damian's only trying to get you out of a hole, Kirby.'

'I know what he's doing,' she flashed back bitterly. 'I *trusted* you,' she said, turning back to Damian. 'I let you have access to confidential information! And all the time you were planning this!'

'If you'll let me continue,' he said quietly, 'you'll see that this isn't nearly as unpalatable as it sounds.'

'You'll become a rich woman, darling,' Wendy put in, pouring the liquid out of an oyster into her mouth. She dabbed her lips. 'You'll probably be a millionairess overnight.'

'I don't want to be a damned millionairess,' she exploded, Wendy's last words landing like petrol on the flames of her anger. 'I'm not interested in money! Just in keeping Keith's business out of the hands of exploiters!'

'The Holt Corporation would not buy Waterford Electronics in order to exploit it,' Damian said, growing cooler as she grew hotter.

'What about those "adjustments" you were talking about the other day? All that stuff about streamlining the company? No doubt your precious steering company will soon put *that* into practice!' Kirby stormed.

'Yes,' he agreed. 'Waterford Electronics needs to be streamlined. Quite apart from anything else, that would disarm the threat from Denison and Braithwaite. But I assure you, Kirby, it can all be achieved without compromising any of your principles.'

'Oh, what rubbish,' she snapped back. 'Listen, Damian. When Roderick Braithwaite told me you wanted to buy out Waterford Electronics, I laughed in his face. I couldn't believe that you were capable of betraying me like that.'

'Kirby——'

'I could have told Roderick then what I'm telling you now: I have no intentions of selling my shares to *anyone*. Least of all to a man who has behaved as you've done!'

'Temper, temper,' Wendy said with her brassy laugh. 'Yorkshire folk are supposed to be an unemotional lot.'

'I've already explained to you,' Damian went on steadily, 'that the principles you think so important would be enshrined in the new company. They'd be written into the charter.'

'And once I lost all control of the company,' she retorted, 'how long would that charter last, Damian? How long before you or your stooges quietly cut out the parts you didn't like?'

'There would be ways of ensuring that didn't happen,' he replied. He, too, was not touching his food any more, in contrast to Wendy, who was finishing off her oysters with considerable relish. 'But obviously there would have to be a certain amount of trust involved.'

'*Trust?*' Kirby said it sharply enough to make diners at other tables glance their way. 'You must be joking. What would be the basis for any trust between us, Damian?'

His eyes met hers with deliberate power. 'The basis would be what we are to each other,' he replied quietly. 'Our friendship.'

She let him hold her gaze for a moment longer, feeling the force of his character. Then she tossed down her napkin, and stood up abruptly.

'I think it stinks, Damian,' she said in a voice that was all the more cutting for its quietness. 'You've betrayed my trust in more ways than I can put words to. You've made a complete fool out of me. But I refuse to be another of your victims. You've had too many victims in your life, from helpless fishermen to big companies. And I want you to know that I think the methods you've stooped to—*all* the methods you've stooped to—are utterly despicable.'

She did not care what Wendy Catchpole made of *that*.

Kirby pushed her chair back, turned on her heel, and walked out of the restaurant in a blind fury. She heard Wendy's coppery laugh behind her.

She crossed the brilliant sunshine of the car park, her blood raging. As she reached the Jaguar, Damian, who must have followed immediately after her, caught up. He grasped her arm, and pulled her round to face him.

'Kirby, don't be a fool,' he said, his face tense.

Her eyes blazed up at him. 'How dare you?' she asked. 'How *dare* you do this to me?'

And they both knew she wasn't just talking about Waterford Electronics.

'It was unavoidable,' he said, obviously answering both questions. 'Not all paths in life are easy. You know that by now.'

'Spare me the philosophy lesson,' she sneered. 'You've chosen your path in life, Damian. And I've chosen mine. And from now on I'd be very grateful if you would stay the hell away from me!'

She tore her arm out of his grasp, and got quickly into the car. Her eyes were so blurred that it was a miracle she didn't hit anything as she accelerated out of the car park.

And then she was speeding away. Speeding home.

She was still holding herself together, somehow, by the time she got back to the Lodge. But she was shaking badly. She went to the kitchen, and made herself a cup of tea, trying to get the trembling under control.

When she'd recovered enough to make some logical judgements about her situation, she knew that she had better start finding out what was happening to Waterford Electronics, fast.

As soon as she judged she was fit to speak to anyone else, she went to the telephone, and started on her enquiries. The first five calls she made were to people whom she knew held smallish blocks of Waterford Electronics shares—the sort of minor shareholders Damian had spoken of targeting.

Of the five, four had already sold their Waterford shares to the Holt Corporation, earlier that week. Small quantities in themselves, ominous regarded as a block.

None of them had thought the matter important enough to warrant telling Kirby.

The fifth, a wealthy local woman of around Kirby's own age, laughed airily. 'Mrs Waterford, I leave all that sort of thing to my broker. I really don't have the brains to make such decisions on my own. He might have sold, for all I know.'

'Well, would you mind if I spoke to him myself?'

'Go ahead, if you must.'

She called the broker, and got the answer she had somehow been expecting.

'Yes, Mrs Waterford. I sold my client's Waterford Electronics holdings just yesterday. Got a good price for them, too, I might add. Holt Corporation are in the big league. Founded by a Braythorpe lad, did you know that?'

'Yes,' she said through clenched teeth. 'I did know that.'

'I assume that, if there's a take-over bid in the offing, it has your personal blessing, Mrs Waterford?'

'I've had no news of a take-over,' she replied calmly. 'Thank you for the information, Mr Blake.'

But she was far from calm as she replaced the receiver. A sensation of frightening impotence was settling over her. It was a Herculean effort to pick up the receiver again, and make a sixth call... to Sir Malcolm Denison.

Malcolm's patrician tones came on the line with a breezy reply.

'Hello there, my dear. I've been wanting to speak to you over these past few days, but you don't seem to be answering your telephone.'

'I've been out rather a lot,' she replied. 'Malcolm, I wanted to speak to you about Waterford Electronics shares.'

'What a coincidence,' came the bland response. 'The very topic I wanted to talk to *you* about.'

'Oh?'

'Yes. I wanted to tell you that I've taken a major decision with regard to Waterford Electronics. I'm pulling out.'

'Pulling out?'

'Cashing in my chips. Between you and Braithwaite and this new force, I really feel there are too many conflicting interests in the company. I don't want to wait until the market price starts dropping. I have my own position to think of.'

'By "this new force", I take it you're referring to the Holt Corporation?' she asked bitterly.

'They're offering an excellent premium,' Sir Malcolm said smugly.

'But you're not seriously thinking of selling? You were Keith's friend!'

'My dear Kirby, business does not run on emotions. And Keith is dead. Now, I tried to give you good advice about Waterford Electronics. You wouldn't listen to me.'

'You wanted the chairmanship, just like Roderick!'

'For the best possible reasons,' he replied smoothly. 'Ever since Keith passed away I've tried to warn you that the firm was becoming increasingly vulnerable. As chairman of Waterford Electronics, I would have said no to Holt. Even if you had taken the measures I suggested months ago, I would perhaps have stayed loyal. But, as it is, I have to look out for my own interests.'

She swallowed, hard. 'May I ask what he has offered?'

'I don't really want to go into that,' came the placid reply. 'But I can say this—nobody could really quibble with the price he's offering. In fact, I can go so far as to say I'm not doing badly out of this at all, Kirby.'

You smarmy little traitor, she thought savagely. I'll bet you aren't. But didn't utter the words. Instead, she forced herself to speak composedly. 'Malcolm, I needn't tell you that I'm opposed to a take-over from Damian Holt. I really feel you owe it to me to give me a first option on your shares. I'll match the Holt Corporation's offer, of course.'

'Ah. And how exactly will you raise the money, Kirby?'

She took a shaky breath. 'I'll sell the Lodge.'

'Well, well,' he said softly. 'So you mean business.'

'Yes, Malcolm. I mean business.'

'Hmm. Well, it's a pity.'

'You've already sold the shares to the Holt Corporation?' she asked in dread.

'Not quite. But I really don't feel I can afford to wait while you put the Lodge on the market, Kirby. It could take months to sell. In the meantime, Waterford Electronics shares might take a nose-dive—especially if there are rumours about a rift in the management.' He sighed in a lifelike imitation of regret. 'No, Kirby, I'm sorry. For my own sake, I'm going to have to let Damian Holt have my shares.'

'I see,' she said numbly. 'You took this decision without consulting me. You didn't even wait until the board meeting next week!'

'Don't sound so distressed,' he said, with phony sympathy. 'Whatever happens, you'll still have a jolly big chunk of the shares. If *you* don't sell to Holt, they can't kick you out—can they?'

'No, but you know as well as I do that I can't control Waterford Electronics on my own. Damian Holt and his people would run rings around me!'

'That *is* rather a problem,' Sir Malcolm sighed in sugary regret.

'Tell me something, Malcolm,' she asked. 'Have you by any chance spoken to Roderick Braithwaite on this topic?'

'Ah, now, Roderick.' Sir Malcolm laughed. 'Roderick Braithwaite is an unpredictable factor. I have no doubt that Holt will have approached him, just as they approached me. But, in addition to being a board member and a major shareholder, Roderick is also chief manager of the firm. And a good chief manager, I might add. He might be a little uncertain about his future in Waterford Electronics, with the Holt Corporation as a major shareholder. I'd guess he'd be pretty ambivalent. If you're considering anything dramatic, like a fight-back, then perhaps Braithwaite is your best ally. Talk it over with him. Personally,' he chuckled, 'I'm just glad to be out of the firing-line, with a good profit in my pocket. Must rush now. Got a golf appointment. Take care, Kirby. Oh—and good luck with that board meeting. I won't be there, of course... but Damian Holt will.' He rang off.

She cried surprisingly little.

Perhaps that was because this was the second time Damian Holt had tried to break her heart, and by now she was getting used to it.

But more likely it was because of the ingredient that hadn't been present six years ago—anger.

Or, to put it more accurately, fury.

It was a shimmering sense of outrage that made Kirby's whole body feel hot. Outrage at the way he'd deceived her about his intentions towards Waterford Electronics. Outrage at the means he'd used to distract her, beguile her, bamboozle her.

All the time she'd been fluttering with excitement at his pretended interest, her poor heart yearning for his affection, he'd been cold-bloodedly setting about a way to take the company away from her. Pluck himself a nice, ripe, profitable plum.

How he must have laughed at her.

He had set about making her fall in love with him, all over again, with scheming deliberation. The kind words. The ride up to Sovereign Force. The caresses that had set her ablaze. All, no doubt, calculated to the last move, the last kiss...

In fact, she thought with a sudden, horrible revelation, Wendy Catchpole's convenient absence itself must have been planned. He had deliberately sent her away to give him a clear field with Kirby Waterford.

Or had she connived at it? She, with her cold green eyes and her 'sophisticated', 'modern' marriage—had she, too, been in on the stratagem?

More than likely. 'We don't let insignificant little details come between us,' she had said. 'We keep our attention on the important things of life.' That had been an almost deliberate taunt. Telling Kirby that she had been used, that she didn't matter, that she was not one of the important things of life.

So, even as Damian had been making love to her, with that apparently blazing passion, there must have remained, somewhere in that over-sized brain of his, an icy little place that never took its attention off the real objective.

How he must have gloated at the way she'd fallen so neatly, so completely into his trap.

That thought made her weep with sheer fury.

Why hadn't she known better? Why had she been so helplessly vulnerable to his wiles? Having once been burned, hadn't she even had the sense to avoid the flame a second time? She cursed her own stupidity with a venom that superseded even her rage against Damian. Fool, idiot, weak-hearted feminine dupe! Was *this* the poise she'd gained over five years of marriage? Was *this* the much-vaunted maturity she'd imagined she had achieved? To let Damian Holt use and abuse her, and then take her company away?

No, she told herself, wiping the tears from her lids. No. She was not going to put her head into that particular noose. Not now. Damian had made the fatal mistake of playing his hand too soon. He should not have let Wendy Catchpole come to that lunch.

It had been Wendy's presence there, more than anything, that had set the alarm bells ringing. Had he chosen to break his great 'plan' to her alone, in the wonderful afterglow of their lovemaking, she might—might just—have fallen for it. Sighed, 'Yes,' and signed on the dotted line.

But now she had seen the pit at her feet, had seen the sharpened stakes of the trap.

Now she'd realised that Damian Holt was not a friend—but an enemy.

When the tears had stopped, Kirby reached for the telephone again. If Roderick Braithwaite was her best ally, then it was time she got in touch with him. Fast.

CHAPTER NINE

CAROLINE LANGTON bent to pick up a stick. She threw it across the meadow, and the dogs went galloping away after it in a babble of enthusiastic yapping.

'Well, if you don't trust Damian Holt,' she said to Kirby, 'I can't imagine how you can think of trusting Roderick Braithwaite. The man is an utter creep.'

'You mean he's not plausible and good-looking, like Damian,' Kirby retorted ironically.

'I mean he's a toad, Kirby! And the fact that you're hob-nobbing with him won't change him into a fairy-prince!'

'I only went to dinner with the man last night—and he *was* one of Keith's oldest friends.'

'He's also a prospective suitor...isn't he?'

'He thought he was. That part wasn't nice, I admit. But I don't have much choice.' Kirby's oval face wore a look of grim determination that her friend had seldom seen on it before. 'At least he'll support me in fighting Damian Holt's take-over. That's all that matters.'

'He'll only support you because he thinks he can make his own position even stronger.'

'I can handle Roderick, Caroline.'

'Can you? And how can you be sure he won't betray you?'

Kirby had no ready answer to that. They crested the rise, and were looking across the fields at Langton Farm. The mellow stone of the old farmhouse was bathed in the late afternoon sunlight. Kirby had come here to her friend's home so many times over the past year. She'd come to regard it as a refuge from storms.

Which was why she was spending another weekend here now, sheltering from the pain of what Damian had done to her. It was a Sunday afternoon, filled with the infinite peace of an English Sunday in the country. She wasn't looking forward to leaving this idyll, and going back to the emptiness of the Lodge tonight.

She thought back over her meeting with Roderick Braithwaite last night at the Braythorpe Hotel. Roderick, of course, had been fully aware of the Holt Corporation take-over bid, and had obviously been waiting—with smug amusement—for her to get back in touch with him.

'I told you what sort of advice Damian Holt likes to give, didn't I, Kirby?' he'd greeted her belligerently. '"Make yourselves nice and small, my lambs, so I can swallow you whole!" Remember? You laughed at me then. You're laughing on the other side of your face now!'

The three hours' discussion which had followed had not been pleasant for Kirby. She'd been forced to eat a great deal of humble pie. Roderick had pointed out, with considerable force, and in several different ways, just how wrong she had been, and just how right he had been.

He'd also repeated his threat to defect to another firm, leaving her to deal with Damian Holt on her own.

But, in the end, drained and exhausted, she had secured what she'd wanted—Roderick's word that he would not sell out to the Holt Corporation, leaving her completely isolated.

In exchange, she had agreed to review Roderick's position within Waterford Electronics. She'd managed to keep that vague, by dint of some very careful arguing;

but they both knew what Roderick was talking about... the chairmanship of the company.

And in the end Kirby knew she was going to have to face up to some very difficult choices. She couldn't keep up this tightrope-walking act indefinitely.

It was Kirby's turn to throw the stick, and she flung it with all her force, deriving some release from the action. The dogs flew after their quarry in joy.

'It seems to me,' Caroline interrupted Kirby's thoughts, 'that you haven't really given Damian Holt anything like a fair chance.'

'Caroline,' she replied drily, 'I know you're a member of the Damian Holt fan club, but how many more chances do I have to give him? I trusted him to find a way of saving Waterford Electronics from exploitation. What he has done is start a take-over bid. It's war, plain and simple.'

'But you haven't listened to his reasoning. By your own admission, you stormed out of L'Escargot in a rage before he'd even finished explaining. You still don't really know the details of what he's offering.'

'I don't have to,' she replied tightly.

They walked homeward, towards the farmhouse. Caroline took her friend's arm. 'Aren't you being rather emotional about this?'

Kirby didn't answer. There was nothing she could say. Caroline did not know what had happened between her and Damian. And Kirby did not want to go into the details of that—not now. It would be too painful, too humiliating, to acknowledge how Damian had led her down the garden path, how he had seduced her mind and body with such contemptuous ease.

The feeling of having been manipulated, violated, was sickening. But she didn't have the heart to reveal her degradation to Caroline yet. So all she said was, 'Maybe

I am being emotional. That doesn't mean I'm not right in what I say.'

'Well, I think you should at least hear what he has to tell you,' Caroline said gently. 'Can't do any harm, can it?'

'I detest him,' Kirby asserted with considerable vehemence. 'I never want to set eyes on him again!'

'Don't you?' Caroline asked gently. 'Well, that's rather unfortunate.'

Kirby looked at her friend in quick dismay. 'Oh, Caroline—you haven't! Have you?'

'If you mean, are you likely to see him again soon . . . the answer is yes.'

'You've invited Damian *here*?' Kirby looked around agitatedly, as if expecting Damian to materialise out of the landscape.

'As a matter of fact, he invited himself here. He seemed to guess that you'd choose my place as your bolt-hole this weekend. He very badly wants to speak to you. A bare three minutes, he said. No more than a word. Naturally, I agreed that he should come and see you here.'

'*Naturally?* How could you, Caroline?'

'I'm a treacherous old hag, I agree. But the man is *very* persuasive, as I'm sure you know. It was hard to resist him. Especially as I'm a member of what you call his fan club.' She held on to Kirby's arm tightly, as though Kirby were liable to bolt, like a rabbit, at any moment. She patted Kirby's hand. 'Personally speaking,' she smiled, 'if a man like Damian Holt were chasing after *me*, I'd be a little more co-operative than you're being.'

Kirby uttered a short word that caused Caroline's eyebrows to rise. 'When is he coming?' she demanded.

Caroline glanced at her watch. 'Actually, he should be at the house right now. I thought I'd get you out of the way while he arrived.'

Kirby stopped dead. She stared blankly at Caroline, then down at her own outfit—shabby cord denims and a scuffed Barbour jacket. She could only guess what the wind had done to her hair and complexion.

'Oh, God,' she sighed. 'And look at the state I'm in.'

Caroline Langton laughed. 'Not very consistent. First you declare you never want to see the man again, now you're worrying about not looking your best to meet him.'

Kirby glared at Caroline. 'I'm glad you think this is funny, Caroline, because I don't! This is awful!'

The older woman made an effort to look solemn. 'Actually, you look fine. You're lucky—you're the type who looks at her best with pink cheeks and tousled hair. Anyway, he's not here to give you marks for fashion. He just wants three minutes' talk with you. Come along, Kirby.'

Kirby groaned as Caroline led her onwards. 'But there's nothing he can say,' she protested. 'I've heard it all before!' The horrible sinking feeling in the pit of her stomach was so very familiar. If she could have turned, and fled across the moorland, she'd have done so. But she was cornered, with no option but to go back into the lion's den.

For the last hundred yards she felt like a prisoner being led to the firing-squad. The feeling wasn't helped by seeing that Damian's black Porsche was indeed parked on the gravel in front of the farmhouse. She was as tense as a drawn bow.

They walked into the house by a side-entrance. Caroline's staff had shown the visitor to the drawing-room, where he was waiting. Kirby wanted to head

straight for her bedroom, to restore at least some order
to her tousled appearance, but Caroline would have none
of it.

'In you go,' she said firmly, pushing Kirby forward.
'I'll leave you in complete privacy.'

'I don't *want* complete—oh, damn! I'll never forgive
you for this, Caroline.'

She took a deep breath, closing her eyes, and tried to
summon her strength. Then she walked into the drawing-
room.

Damian was standing in front of the fire, a tall, dark
figure in casual clothes that emphasised his splendid
physique. He did not move as she came into the room.
But the deep blue eyes met hers with an impact that was
like an electric shock.

He was silent for a moment, just studying her. Then
he said, 'I've been trying to telephone you since Friday,
Kirby.'

She forced herself to speak. 'I told Mrs Carstairs to
ignore your calls.'

'And not tell me where you were when I came to the
Lodge,' he said drily. 'Yes, I know.'

Her voice stuck in her dry throat. 'I asked you to stay
away from me, Damian. Why did you come here?'

'Because, despite what you may believe, you and I
have a great deal to discuss, Kirby.'

'Such as?' she asked tautly.

'The *least* important issue is the fact that I am now
rapidly becoming a major shareholder in your company.
I'm already entitled to a seat on the board. That alone
requires us to do some talking, wouldn't you say?'

Her voice was hard. 'Oh, I know what you want to
discuss.'

'Do you?'

'Of course. You're buying up all the spare shares you can find. You've even managed to talk Sir Malcolm Denison into betraying me. But you won't have full control until you've got your hands on the shares Keith left me. *That's* why you're here, Damian. Even though you know I've seen through you and the hateful game you've played with me. Well, we can do all the talking we need to do at the board meeting.'

'Kirby,' he said quietly, 'I can understand your anger. What I can't understand is why you won't even let me speak to you.'

'So you can tell me more lies?'

'I've never lied to you.'

'You betrayed me,' Kirby flashed. 'You behaved in the most despicable way a man can ever behave towards a woman.'

'And how is that?' he asked.

'You violated my trust! You took me to bed and made love to me to blind me to what you were doing behind my back!'

'Do you really think that?' he asked, his eyes holding hers. 'Is that why you think I took you to bed and made love to you?'

'I don't think it was out of charity to a poor widow,' she said, her cheeks scarlet now. 'When you were se-ducing me, Damian, you had already begun buying up Waterford shares. In secret. Without telling me. Do you really expect me to imagine your intentions were pure as the driven snow?'

'I didn't have what you call "intentions" of any kind,' he replied, even more quietly. 'We made love because that was what we'd both been longing for from the moment we set eyes on one another again...right here, in this room.'

'Very romantic,' she replied shortly, trying to disguise the way his quiet words had affected her.

'We made love,' he went on, 'because we *are* in love. And have been so ever since we were little more than children.'

That hit her like a dagger stabbing into her heart. She went pale, and felt the room sway around her. 'How can you be so cruel?' she whispered.

'As for my not telling you about the shares—how could I? I'd already developed the only plan I could see for achieving what you wanted. I started to tell you what I had in mind up at Sovereign Force. But before I could get to the point you said that you would never dream of selling Waterford Electronics to me. You said you trusted me even less than Braithwaite or Denison. You said you could never believe me capable of an altruistic action. I realised then that it would be better to present you with a *fait accompli* than try and convince you by reasoning.'

'Well, you've presented me with your *fait accompli*, all right. But you're not going to have it all your own way,' she told him grimly. 'I'm not as defenceless as you hope I am.'

'You mean Roderick Braithwaite?' Damian shrugged. 'I know you saw him last night. I can imagine what you discussed. But, I assure you, he doesn't come into this.'

'He comes into it more than you might like to think,' she retorted. 'Between us, Roderick and I still control the majority of the stock.'

Damian's tanned face was as immobile as if graven from bronze. 'Roderick Braithwaite is too sensible to oppose what is clearly the best course for the company,' he said.

'Perhaps Roderick Braithwaite has motives which you don't know about,' she said recklessly.

She saw Damian's eyes narrow quickly. 'Oh? What motives are those?'

'I told you. Roderick wants to marry me. I'm going to accept him.'

'What rubbish!'

'It is *not* rubbish,' she flung at him. 'As a matter of fact, we set the date last night!'

She had the satisfaction of seeing the naked anger detonate in Damian's normally controlled face. He reached her in two swift paces, his fingers biting into her arms with enough force to make her gasp with pain. His eyes blazed down at her like dark lightning. 'Tell me you don't mean that,' he said in a voice whose controlled savagery made her skin tingle.

'You're hurting me, Damian,' she told him, finding a quiet dignity somewhere within the turmoil of her emotions. 'And of course I mean it. I mean everything I say—unlike you.'

'You cannot marry that man,' he grated.

'Why not?' she asked. 'He's a superb manager.'

'He might be a Nobel prize-winning economist, for all I care. He's not a fit husband for you!'

This time it was Kirby's turn to grow cooler as he grew hotter. 'Let me go, please,' she commanded. 'I refuse to talk to you while you're mauling me.'

He stared into her face for a moment. Then the disturbing pressure of those strong fingers eased. But he did not release her. Instead, he drew her against his broad chest, his arms sliding around her shoulders to hold her in a close embrace.

She could not restrain her shudder of emotion as she felt him kiss her throat, his hands caressing her as though he were a groom gentling a distressed thoroughbred. 'Kirby,' she heard him murmur, his mouth close to her ear, 'I'm sorry you had to suffer...I didn't intend it.'

Then he let her go, and took a step back. By the taut expression on his face, he was fighting down emotions every bit as wild and conflicting as the ones now raging in her own heart.

'I have very little time right now,' he went on, with an effort. 'I have to take Wendy to the airport in a few minutes. She's flying back down to London this afternoon.'

'To give you another crack at the merry widow?' she asked cruelly.

'No. For good. Wendy and I have broken off our engagement.'

Kirby tried not to show him how sickeningly her heart had lurched at those words. 'If you expect me to believe *that*,' she retorted, 'you must take me for an even bigger fool than I thought.'

'Whatever you believe,' he replied, recovering his self-control, 'it's the truth.' Damian glanced at his watch. 'I have to go. But before I do I want you to agree to meet me again. And I want you to promise you'll listen to what I have to say about Waterford Electronics. Whatever the future holds for us, we evidently have to get that out of the way before you'll be able to think straight. Will you promise me you'll listen? And that you'll trust me, Kirby?'

Her mind was still battling to grasp the news about Wendy Catchpole. Could it be true? She took a shaky breath. 'When do you want to meet?'

'I'll come and pick you up at the Lodge tomorrow lunchtime. Agreed?'

She stared at him, feeling as though a maelstrom was whirling inside her, opposing emotions battling wildly for supremacy. It was an effort to speak at last. 'How can I ever believe you, Damian?' she asked in a tortured voice. 'How do I know whether you're telling me the truth or callous lies?'

'I don't think I can give you the answer to that, Kirby,' he replied gently. 'I think the answer lies in your own heart.'

He leaned forward, and kissed her on the mouth. She made no effort to avoid him. His lips were warm and possessive, but the contact was momentary. Then he was walking out of the room, without turning back.

Kirby felt so weak that she had to sit down. She hugged her aching stomach with both arms, hunched by the fire, whose warmth did not seem to touch her. Fragments of what he had said whirled through her mind like leaves in a gale...We are in love...and have been so ever since we were little more than children...trust me, Kirby.

Of course, she had been lying when she'd said she had accepted Roderick's proposal. They hadn't even discussed the idea on Saturday night—Roderick knew that particular scheme was a dead duck. It had never been anything else, whatever she might have led Damian to believe.

But she'd been almost shocked by the raw anger with which he'd reacted to those words. Damian was not given to displays of emotion, but there had been no doubt of his passion then. Had she totally misjudged him? Were there true and deep emotions beneath that composed male façade?

She heard Caroline come into the room, and felt the gentle touch of her friend's hand on her shoulder. 'Kirby—are you all right?'

'No,' she said unevenly. 'I'm not all right. I've never felt so lost in all my life, Caroline.'

Caroline sat beside her. 'What did he want?'

'He wants to see me again, alone. To explain about Waterford Electronics, he says. But he said other things, too. That he's broken off his engagement to Wendy. But I can't believe him...'

'Don't cry,' Caroline urged, as Kirby broke down. 'I trust him, even if you don't. I'd trust him with my life. Can't you trust him with a little of your time?'

Kirby fought for control over herself. She found a handkerchief, and dried her eyes. 'Doesn't look as though I've got much choice, does it?' she said bitterly.

'No,' Caroline agreed with a smile. 'It doesn't.'

Monday dawned grey, windy and rainy again. The fine autumn days were steadily giving way to less pleasant winter weather. Braythorpe could hardly be seen for the pall of mist that hung over the town, and up here a stiff northerly was stripping petals from the last roses with ferocious glee.

The Lodge was especially sombre on days like this. The high-ceilinged rooms were full of shadows, no matter how many lights were on. The wind moaned in the eaves. An atmosphere of cold and melancholy pervaded the house, a sort of unheard lament, whose refrain was the tap-tap of the roses against the windows.

Kirby had been awake since six. She lay in bed, no longer asleep, but not yet ready to face the day, haunted by intensely felt but unclear thoughts. It all tumbled around in her brain, like garments in a washing machine—Damian, the firm, her own future, Roderick Braithwaite, Wendy Catchpole...

The prospect of joining forces with Roderick against a take-over by Damian was not alluring. True, between the two of them, she and Roderick would always have a significant proportion of the stock, however many Damian managed to secure. But not a big enough majority to fight him off. And, as she'd told Caroline, she had no hope of being able to control the future of Waterford Electronics the way she'd been doing so far.

That capacity was already gone. She had to recognise that. Even if Roderick had been a pliable person, who would do exactly as she ordered all the time, the presence of Damian within the firm would be intolerable. His brilliance and authority would soon dominate them all.

And Roderick was *not* a pliable ally. He had definite ideas about the future of Waterford Electronics, and, to keep him on her side, she would have to make bigger and bigger concessions to his ideas. And in the process she would lose all control over Waterford Electronics. One way or the other, she was being forced into a corner.

Like Hercules, she remembered from her schooldays, forced to sail between the two perils of Scylla and Charybdis—the whirlpool and the monster.

And there were deeper, more disturbing implications in all this.

That Damian, her whirlpool, had broken off his engagement with Wendy Catchpole was the most disturbing factor among so many in all her turbulent thoughts.

Was it true? And, if it was, could she really believe the implication that Damian wanted *her*?

He had hurt her so badly once before. If only she could learn to trust him again . . . but could she ever trust him again? It was just too much to ask, to throw herself back into the whirlpool for his sake.

And yet . . . was she being blind to her own emotions? How long could she keep denying the strength of her own bond with Damian?

It was there, like the living force within a tree. No matter how many times she tried to lop off its branches, it was continually putting forth new leaves, new flowers. A force that was constantly renewed, fed from roots that went deep, deep into her being. It would only fade when she herself did. She knew that now.

If it had survived five years of marriage to Keith, with Damian far away in London, what would happen now that they were both free? How could she stop those beautiful, treacherous blossoms from bursting out?

It was something she could no longer deceive herself about. She had pretended and dissembled for too long now. The time was coming when she would have to face up to it—her enduring, absolute love for Damian.

She'd once been foolish enough to imagine that she had outgrown it. But she'd been wrong. So very wrong. It had grown, as she had grown. She loved him more, now, than she had done six years ago.

Then she had loved him as a girl, with a girl's inexperience, a girl's inability to cope with big emotions. Now she loved him as a mature woman. She loved him as someone who understood what love was. Why could she not just accept that? Let the whirlpool draw her in, deep, deep...abandon all hope...just let Damian do as he pleased with her?

Kirby rose, feeling as though there was a fire in her head. She showered and dressed, and went downstairs to face the day.

She had already finished her simple breakfast of fruit and coffee before Mrs Carstairs and her two helpers arrived. She greeted them warmly, as usual, but the elderly housekeeper seemed to sense the melancholy mood of the house.

'It's a gloomy place on a day like this,' she said to Kirby as she put on her apron. 'These old houses need families in them to bring them alive. A person on their own can never fill all the empty spaces.'

Mrs Carstairs had dropped hints like this before, and Kirby just nodded an absent agreement. But she was surprised when the housekeeper went on in forthright fashion, 'This'll be your second winter here all on your own, ma'am. A year alone in the Lodge is quite enough. Don't you fancy somewhere a little cosier...more suitable for a lady in your position?'

'You mean—get rid of the Lodge?'

'Aye, that's what I do mean.' Mrs Carstairs poured herself a cup of coffee from the percolator Kirby had prepared. 'Even when Mr Waterford was alive, this house was far too big. If you'd had a family, now...but that wasn't to be. And, since he passed away, God rest him, it's been nothing but a burden to you, Mrs Waterford. Isn't that true?'

Kirby studied the sensible old face. 'Are you saying the place is getting too much for you, Mrs Carstairs?'

'Well, it certainly is that,' Mrs Carstairs agreed with Yorkshire directness. 'But that wasn't what I was getting at.' She stirred her coffee briskly, looking at Kirby sideways.

Kirby smiled, despite her heavy heart, and pulled a chair back. 'Sit down, Mrs Carstairs, and tell me what you *were* getting at.'

The housekeeper sat down, smoothing her severe white apron with her hands. 'There've been rumours in the town,' she began. 'Rumours about Waterford Electronics. They say the firm is likely to be coming under new management soon. Now, I don't understand the ins and outs of high finance, ma'am, but everyone knows Mr Holt's a fine gentleman.'

'Do they?' she prompted warily.

'Aye, they do.' Mrs Carstairs sipped her coffee. 'And he's a Braythorpe lad, though he lives in London these days. They trust him to run the firm just as Mr Waterford would have done. Now, some folks say that you're not keen on his taking over. They say you think of it as...well, as sort of disloyal to your late husband's memory. But that would be a silly way to think, wouldn't it?'

'You tell me,' Kirby invited drily. 'I don't know.'

'Well, it's obvious. A woman who's had no experience of business shouldn't be expected to take over where her husband left off. It isn't right. It's too much of a burden. Sooner or later she has to find a suitable man to carry on. That's what *I* say, ma'am.'

'You're telling me to sell the Lodge and let Damian Holt take over Waterford Electronics?' Kirby said.

'I wouldn't presume to tell you how to run your life, Mrs Waterford.'

'But that's what you *are* saying. In fact, you're asking me to do you out of a job, among other things.'

There was a twinkle in the wise old eyes. 'If you're worried about the staff——' she jerked her thumb in the direction of the maids '—*they'll* find new jobs soon enough. As for me, I'm about ready to retire.' She paused to drain her cup. 'Or, if I was wanted to continue in the same position, but in a smaller house,' she continued casually as she rose to her feet, 'there might be a few years left in me yet.'

'I'll bear that in mind,' Kirby smiled.

'One more thing, ma'am.'

'What's that?'

'A lovely young woman oughtn't to stay a widow. It's not seemly. A year of mourning is enough. It's time to think about picking up your life again. I'll be about my business now, ma'am.'

Kirby sat alone, looking broodingly out at the rain. How tempting. How very tempting to abdicate her responsibilities towards Waterford Electronics on to broader, stronger shoulders. How very tempting to leave the Lodge and its echoing rooms, and move to a single-woman-sized apartment in Braythorpe.

Somewhere warm and bright. With a view of the river, perhaps. Within reach of the cheerful bustle of the town. Somewhere she would be able to see her old friends for coffee, meet people of her own age, recover her stalled life...

But, at the moment, those were impossible dreams.

She turned to the mountain of correspondence, social and business, that she had to work on this morning.

But she was still fantasising about this prospect several hours later when she realised, with a sinking sensation of panic, that Damian would soon be here to pick her up.

She hastened to get ready. The wintry weather dictated warm clothes. She chose a roll-neck jersey in downy, dove-grey wool, and a pair of matching wool trousers, tucked into a pair of soft leather boots that would withstand the worst of the slush. A hat and coat were going to be a necessity if they had to walk anywhere.

She applied make-up with a light hand, as she always did. She studied her own pale face in the mirror as she touched her lips with red. She looked so tired and frail. These past days had drained her emotions. She had not felt this kind of emotional exhaustion since... She smiled wearily. Since the last time Damian had derailed her life.

She snapped the lipstick shut, and brushed the chestnut curls of her hair. Whether it was because she had slept badly, or because of the cumulative drain on her feelings, today she felt close to capitulation. Coming on top of everything else, Mrs Carstairs's enticing picture of a life without the nightmare burdens of the Lodge and the firm had affected her strongly.

She wished with all her heart that she looked prettier to face Damian this morning. The pathetic wishes of a woman in love, she thought wryly. Wanting to be more beautiful, more attractive, more irresistible.

Come on, Kirby, she told herself fiercely. Don't be a weak fool. Pull yourself together, girl!

She was getting increasingly nervous. She had to force herself to stop drumming her fingers or showing other signs of nerves as she waited downstairs. She pretended to be busy with her correspondence, but in reality was far too highly strung to concentrate on anything.

If she could have avoided this coming interview by any means possible, she would have done. But she knew Damian's character. He would not give up until he had achieved his goal. She would have to face him, and get this over with, once and for all.

Mrs Carstairs tapped at the door. 'A telephone call for you, ma'am. A Miss Catchpole, from London.'

Kirby stiffened. It was on the tip of her tongue to tell Mrs Carstairs to say she was out. But then curiosity overcame her reservations. She went to the telephone, and lifted it.

'Kirby Waterford speaking,' she said briskly.

The familiar, upper-class tones replied, 'Hello, Kirby. It's Wendy Catchpole. I'm calling from my flat, in London.' There was a pause. 'I don't know whether Damian's told you about our various decisions yet.'

'He mentioned that you had gone back down to London,' Kirby answered guardedly.

'Ah. Well, there's more to it than that, though I expect Damian will tell you about that himself, in time. There are various ramifications, business and personal. But I'm making this call on my own behalf. To give you a little business advice, woman to woman.'

'Oh, yes?' Kirby said, her voice growing even stiffer. 'I seem to be getting a lot of business advice lately.'

'You need it,' Wendy said bluntly. 'You know very little about business, despite the position that your husband's death has put you in.' The tones were as clipped and precise as ever, but Kirby sensed no underlying hostility beneath Wendy's speech. 'I'm not going to be wearisome about this. But I feel there are one or two things you really ought to know about Damian.'

'I don't think you can tell me anything I don't already know about Damian,' she replied shortly.

'Don't be too sure. You've known him a lot longer than I have, I agree. But you know him as a man. *I* know him as a businessman. And that's a very different matter. I see things about him that you don't.'

'Such as?' Kirby challenged.

'To take an example, you seem rather fixated on this wretched affair of the polluted river... the chemical spillage, the poisoned fish—all that little drama.'

'Is there something I don't know about that?'

'Kirby, business runs on other people's money. Shareholders' money. You understand that, surely. A company loss is the shareholders' loss. When a chemical firm gets sued for millions, it isn't just some faceless corporation—it's thousands of individuals, some of them by no means rich, who stand to make a loss.'

'Nothing like the loss of those fishermen, who had their livelihood taken away from them!'

'Damian didn't spill the chemicals himself, you know,' Wendy replied mildly. 'It was an accident. Accidents do happen. But what I'm trying to get at is that it was Damian's primary duty, as head of the group, to make sure that his shareholders didn't suffer an unacceptable loss. He had an obligation to them which came before his obligation to outside parties, even though they'd also sustained a serious misfortune.'

'I'm not as naïve as all that, Wendy,' she retorted. 'I know that argument.'

'Yes. But what you don't know is that, once he'd successfully contested the fishermen's claim, he paid for the clean-up out of his own pocket.'

'What?'

'He would never talk about it, perhaps not even to you. He values his ruthless image far too highly. It keeps his shareholders confident that he'll always defend their interests to the utmost. But I can tell you for a fact that he paid over two million pounds of his own money to finance the clean-up—in addition to setting up a trust fund to help the fishing villages over the crisis.'

Kirby was too stunned to answer for a moment. 'Is that—is that true?' she stammered at last.

'It's not only true, but the aid programme is set to continue for several more years yet. They'll be able to buy new boats, new nets, and improve their standard of living dramatically. I'm not trying to make Damian out as some kind of angel. But I hate to hear him criticised by people who don't know any better. Like that man at Caroline's party. As I said then, the Holt Corporation is one of the most generous organisations of its size in the world. Damian gives away millions to Third World countries each year. He has a lot of dreams about world unity and the elimination of poverty... things that his competitors would laugh themselves sick at.'

'I—I can hardly believe all this!'

'Why would I lie to you?' Wendy laughed, her metallic voice taking on a wry quality. 'Do you think it suits me to be whitewashing Damian's character to my worst rival, Kirby? I'm not a person given to strong emotions. But if I were ever to hate someone, you would qualify at the top of the list.'

'I've said some awful things to him,' Kirby said numbly. 'I feel terrible now.'

'Oh, I wouldn't worry about that. As I said, Damian rather relishes his image as the remorseless capitalist, grinding the faces of the poor. It amuses him . . . and it's good business. He's really rather a softie, inside.'

This extraordinary telephone call had cut Kirby's legs from beneath her. She sat down, feeling slightly unsteady. 'Why have you called to tell me all this?'

'Well, it's my roundabout way of getting to the problem of your own company, Waterford Electronics. By the way you reacted the other day, you've swallowed the Damian Holt myth hook, line and sinker. Don't let other people do your thinking for you, Kirby. Check the facts for yourself.'

'How can I do that?'

'Ask people who know. For that matter, ask Damian himself. If he really cares about you, he might let you see the man behind the mask. Now, you asked Damian to help you with your company, and he's doing just that. But you're still wearing blinkers. You're seeing him as some kind of ogre. He isn't. If he says he can guarantee to keep your company user-friendly, then he will. After all,' she pointed out gently, 'he has had some experience in that field. Furthermore, put yourself on the scale of things. I know Waterford Electronics is a fair-sized firm, but it's really a very small affair compared to the organisations Damian runs. It really wouldn't be worth his while to take over your firm just to run it into the ground. If he weren't so very—fond of you, he wouldn't be doing any of this.'

'I don't know what to say, Wendy.' Kirby rubbed her face. 'I really don't know what to say.'

'Well, that's about it. Hope you'll forgive me for sticking my nose in.'

'You've been—I want to thank you, Wendy.'

'Not at all. I hate a muddle. Can't bear turmoil of any kind. It's such a waste of time and energy, isn't it?'

'I suppose you're right...'

'I wonder,' Wendy said as she rung off, 'whether you have any idea how lucky you are, Kirby.'

Kirby put the telephone down, her head spinning. Suddenly, everyone was telling her what a wonderful person Damian Holt was. As if she needed telling...

And at last she heard the growl of Damian's Porsche outside the house. She rose, and went to the door to greet him.

CHAPTER TEN

DAMIAN was wearing a dark suit, with a supple suede coat thrown over his wide shoulders. He looked what he was—distinguished, successful, an achiever. He greeted her on the doorstep, unsmiling.

'Good morning, Kirby.'

'Good morning, Damian.' She looked at him, wondering whether she would ever see a more beautiful man as long as she lived.

'Got a coat?' he asked. 'Good. Let's go.'

'Where are you taking me?' she asked, as he held open the door of the Porsche.

'To lunch,' was all he replied. He had not kissed her, but he took her arm as they walked to his car. The hard muscles of his body brushed against her, setting her emotions fluttering.

As they drove down the road towards the town, she remembered, with an acute pang, the drive back from the stables on the afternoon of their ride to Sovereign Force. Then they'd been on their way, though she hadn't known it then, to an unforgettable night of love. Then, too, it had been wet and rainy. Perhaps rain was the weather that suited them best...

She turned in her seat to look at him. 'Bought any more Waterford Electronics shares this morning?' she asked with light irony.

'A few more,' he replied. 'With all the interest, the price is starting to rise, unfortunately. This could work out an expensive exercise. Unless...'

'Unless?' she prompted as he paused.

'Unless I can talk you into letting me have yours cheap.'

She was so taken aback by this audacity that she snorted. He turned to her with that hidden smile of his. 'Don't bother saying what's in your mind,' he said. 'I can guess.'

She took a deep breath. 'Did you get Wendy to the airport on time?' she asked sweetly.

'Yes,' he nodded. 'We parted very amicably.'

'What about dear Daddy? Isn't he going to be upset that this oh, so convenient love-match isn't coming off?'

'Gerald? I've already spoken to him. He's no more heartbroken than Wendy is.'

'Even after you jilted his daughter?'

'He understands. You have to realise,' Damian said evenly, 'that my relationship with Wendy had very little in common with, say, my relationship with you. It was never based on emotion. It was far more like a business deal. If you don't marry for love,' he shrugged, 'you might as well marry for more mercenary reasons.'

'And you're a very mercenary man, aren't you, Damian?' she said.

'My options were limited,' he replied gently. 'I knew I would never marry for love. Wendy was a good choice. . . while other options were closed. It would have suited us all for economic reasons. You called it a merger the other day, and you weren't far wrong. But when other factors came into it the economics just weren't relevant any more.'

'As a matter of fact,' Kirby said casually, 'Wendy rang me this morning, just before you arrived.'

He looked at her sharply. 'What did she say?'

'Oh. . . this and that. We discussed your character.'

'This is beginning to sound more and more sinister.'

'There were a few surprises. When you told me you and she had broken up yesterday, I didn't really believe you. But from what she said on the telephone, I don't seem to have much choice any more.'

'You thought I was lying?'

'I don't know what I thought. When did you make this decision?'

'For my part? One minute after I set eyes on you last weekend.'

She closed her eyes. How skilful he was at knowing where to thrust the dagger in! If he only knew his capacity to wound her vulnerable emotions! 'You should write romantic movie-scripts, Damian. You have a definite talent for flummery.'

He did not respond to the gibe, perhaps sensing that it held no bitterness. 'You're different this morning,' he said.

'In what way?'

'Well, for one thing, you're not at my throat the whole time. What's changed, Kirby?'

'I'm not quite sure,' she replied slowly. 'Maybe I have.'

'Did Wendy say something to alter your opinion of me?'

'No, not really. My opinion of you is pretty much fixed, Damian. It was fixed a long time ago, and nothing will ever really change it.'

'Sounds ominous,' he smiled.

'Wendy's call was...' She hesitated. 'Sometimes, in the mornings, you're lying awake, but still dreamy—and the alarm goes off. It hasn't really awoken you, but it's a signal that you have to face up to reality now. That's what Wendy's call was like.' She turned her face away from him, looking out of the window of the car. They were driving along a leafy lane that ran parallel to the river, leading to a secluded residential area where some of Braythorpe's grandest houses were situated. 'Where are we going?' she said. 'There are no restaurants around here.'

'I thought we'd take a look at something before we ate,' he said cryptically. 'Right here, in fact.'

Kirby saw the name of the house as he swung the Porsche into the driveway. It was picked out on the massive wrought-iron gates that hung open on stone pillars—Ely Hall. She also saw a 'For Sale' sign beneath it. She sat in silent puzzlement as they approached the house through an avenue of giant chestnut trees.

Ely Hall, when it came into view, was not huge. But the stunning beauty of its ivy-clad façade made Kirby gasp. It was perfectly proportioned, an English country house of immaculate loveliness.

An old house. Older than the Lodge, older even than Langton Farm, this majestic house must have dated back to the early seventeenth century, at least. Its gables and barley-twist chimneys proclaimed that.

As they approached, she saw that the front garden was filled with topiary figures, yew bushes clipped into fantastic shapes of animals and birds, every leaf trimmed to precision over centuries of skill.

'What are we doing here?' she asked Damian in astonishment.

'Don't you like the place?'

'I love it. It's the most beautiful house I've ever seen. But I still don't know what we're doing here...' She gazed around. 'The place looks deserted. And there was a "For Sale" sign at the gate, wasn't there?'

Damian parked the car in front of Ely Hall, and took something out of his pocket, holding it up for her to see. 'The keys,' he said succinctly.

'I can see that. Keys to what? To *this* place?'

The smile that never reached his mouth was in his eyes again. 'Yes. To this place. Let's take a look.'

Kirby followed him in bewilderment to the front door. He unlocked it, and she tentatively went in.

The serene atmosphere of the lovely old house enveloped them. She paused in the hallway, gazing up at the carved minstrel gallery that ran above their heads. Ely Hall, was, if that were possible, even more beautiful inside than out. She caught an impression of magnificent old furniture, fine oil-paintings, Persian rugs on the floor. Carved linenfold panelling ran the entire length of the hall. A splendid chandelier hung from the ceiling, its crystal prisms muted now, as if waiting to fulminate into dazzling light at the touch of a switch.

Damian was standing beside her, watching the expressions cross her face. She turned to him at last, shaking her head. 'Damian, what on earth are we doing here? Why have you brought me to this house?'

'To get your opinion.'

'You're thinking of making an investment? Here?'

'I want to buy this house. To live in.'

Her throat was constricted again. 'I didn't know you were thinking of moving back to Braythorpe.'

'I've more or less decided,' he said casually. 'These days I can keep in touch with my business interests via telephone, cable or fax. I don't need to be in London any more. I'm getting tired of city life. And I'm getting tired of my bachelor flat. I was starting to long for my roots, for something a little more...permanent.'

'Well, this is permanent all right,' she said, as they moved onward through the house. 'It's been here around four hundred years already. God, it's beautiful—look at that stonework. And that fireplace looks like genuine Adam. The furniture is fabulous.'

'That's for sale, too. The family who own it now are wealthy Middle Easterners. They've never used it, and now they want to sell up, furnishings included. Some of the pieces were made especially for the house when it was built, around 1620, by the Ely family.'

Kirby glanced at him. 'It *is* rather a jump from a bachelor flat, Damian. Mrs Carstairs was telling me only this morning that a big house is no more than a burden to a single person.'

'True. But I'm not planning to live here alone. I'm planning to share the house with the woman I love…and our children.' He said this while gazing thoughtfully round the room, but Kirby felt her heart lurch. 'As a matter of fact,' he added absently, 'it's just the right size for a growing family…wouldn't you say?'

Unperturbed by the fact that Kirby did not answer, he led her upstairs. The bedrooms were large and airy, with luxurious modern bathrooms en suite. The master bedroom was huge, and had a massive bay window whose leaded panes looked down on to the topiary garden, to the lush fields beyond, and to the soft hills of Yorkshire beyond them. It was a view that took her breath away.

'The land extends beyond those woods,' he told her, pointing at a distant blaze of autumn colours. 'It comes to around thirty or forty acres in all.'

'This property must be astronomically expensive,' she said, finding her voice at last.

'It isn't cheap, no. But I'm not a poor man, Kirby. And, when you're buying a house that will be your home for the rest of your life, and your children's home after you…well, price doesn't come into it.'

She traced the lead of the panes with her fingertips. 'Don't you think,' she asked quietly, 'that this is putting unfair pressure on me?'

'Pressure?' he asked innocently.

'Pressure to get me to say yes.'

She heard his soft laugh. 'I haven't asked you anything yet.'

'Yes, you have.' She turned and met his eyes. 'Did you think I wouldn't accept you without this house as a make-weight?'

He moved to her, his expression changing subtly. 'Judging from the last couple of interviews we've had, I wouldn't bank on your accepting me if I locked you up in a lighthouse for twenty years.' He took her hands in his, his strong fingers twining round hers. 'Well?' he asked, slate-blue eyes searching hers with profound enquiry. '*Would* you accept me without this house as a make-weight?'

Her fingers tightened around his. 'Damian,' she whispered, 'you were always too good to be true. I've loved you half my life without ever being able to hope that this moment would come true. And now...'

'And now?'

'I've been blind about you, Damian. Blind to your true character. Oh, it wasn't Wendy's phone call, though that helped me face up to the truth. Even if you *were* the exploitative monster I tried to pretend you were, I'd still have been yours... helplessly yours.'

She saw the emotion move, deep within his eyes. 'Kirby, I don't deserve you. The mistake I made six years ago was so terrible that I can hardly bear to think of it now... When you married Keith Waterford, it was as though my heart stopped beating. As though my emotions, all of me, went into some kind of suspended animation. For the first couple of years, I lived in hope that the marriage wouldn't work. I lived in hope of a separation, a divorce... God forgive me, but I couldn't believe you could ever be happy with another man. But you stayed married. And you seemed to love Keith. And I had to face the fact that you *could* be happy with another man, and that I'd made the biggest miscalculation of my entire life.'

' "Happy",' she said quietly. 'That's a word with so many meanings, Damian. Sometimes we use it just to mean that we're not suffering.' She searched his face, that beautiful face she knew better than her own, that had been in her dreams ever since she could remember. 'We almost never use it to mean what it really ought to mean—true joy, the feeling that so many people only have for one or two moments. I wasn't happy with Keith. It's not disloyal to his memory to say that any more. I didn't love him. And a woman can only know happiness with the man she loves. Keith was very kind, a wonderful man in so many ways. But all he could ever do was stop me from suffering. *Happiness*...that's what you make me feel, Damian. Even when you're breaking my heart.'

He smiled with a touch of sadness. 'I can't even say I wasn't suffering. I was. All those years. Oh, yes, I've been brilliantly successful, the whiz-kid of the decade. From the outside, I do a good impression of a dynamic human being who speaks and walks and achieves things. But inside, where it mattered, I wasn't really alive at all. I'd destroyed the most important part of myself in a moment of folly. All the rest—the money, the success, the razzmatazz—none of it really mattered a damn. I drifted into that engagement without hope, without any expectations of love or joy. I'd left all that behind me six years ago. But when I saw you again at Caroline Langton's house, and you told me Keith was dead...' he shook his head '...it was like an earthquake. I don't know how else to describe it. Everything seemed to crumble around me. I didn't dare hope—and yet I no longer felt that crushing sense of despair.'

They moved unthinkingly to the bed, and sat facing one another, their fingers still locked together.

'I told Wendy how I felt the next day,' Damian went on. 'I was completely open with her. We never pre-

tended to be in love with one another, and, whatever
her failings, Wendy is a very honest person. She knew
that I had always loved you. When I told her that, with
you now free, I couldn't marry her, she wasn't heartbroken. But she suggested we give each other a week to
see whether it was the right decision. I felt I had to agree,
even though I had no doubt about the way I felt. That's
why she went back to London on Monday. When she
came back, she knew at once that I'd been right. I was
in love with you, and I could never marry anyone else.'

Kirby swallowed, trying to ease the choking sensation
of breathlessness that had overcome her.

Damian went on, 'She insisted on coming to
L'Escargot on Friday to take what she called "a last look
at the conqueror". You can't blame her for needling you
a little over that lunch. After you stormed out, as a
matter of fact, she told me I was a very lucky man. She
called you a very classy lady, which is probably the
biggest compliment Wendy can give. She knew then why
I loved you so much.'

Kirby couldn't speak for a moment. 'She told me the
real facts behind that pollution business this morning,'
she said at last. 'How you used your own money to put
things right. When I was so sharp with you…why didn't
you just put me over your knee? And then tell me the
truth?'

He laughed. 'I'm not proud of myself, Kirby. Paying
up was the least I could do. That chemical spillage was
a disaster. I had to protect my shareholders, but I
couldn't have let those people suffer, either. I felt terrible. Despite the corporate image, my politics are more
green than any other colour.'

'And your plans for Waterford Electronics…the most
minor of your recent acquisitions? I've been wrong about
those, too, haven't I?'

'You haven't shown the best judgement in the world,' he said solemnly.

'No... perhaps not. But I'm showing it now.'

'Are you?'

'Yes,' she said decisively, sliding her arms around his neck. 'Because I'm not going to let you get away again, Damian.'

His mouth was so close to hers that she could feel its warmth touch her, sending her pulses racing. 'Does this mean you'll marry me?' he whispered.

'Well, now,' she hedged. 'I can't make any promises, but——'

His mouth silenced her.

The moment had no end. The silence of the untenanted house was gentle, somehow welcoming, as though it were wistful for the emotional warmth that had been missing for so long. Kirby ran her hands slowly across Damian's shoulders, tracing the precise symmetry of his muscles. Their tongues caressed with slow, gentle tenderness, until the first flare of desire awoke, like a flame that never died down completely.

'I love you, Kirby,' he whispered. 'Haven't you made me suffer enough already?'

'Not nearly enough,' she laughed huskily. 'You don't think I'm going to give in just like that, do you?'

He drew her close, burying his face against her throat hungrily. She moaned softly as she felt the sweet torment of his lips against her throbbing pulse. The wonderful magic was casting its spell all over again, setting fire to her nerve-ends, making her heart thud like a pagan drum.

She ran her fingers through his crisp, dark hair, glorying in the sheer sensuality of him. He lifted the soft wool of her sweater gently, and bent to kiss the soft curve of her breasts.

Kirby whispered his name, cradling his head as he tasted her scented skin, his mouth seeking the hardening peaks of her nipples. Desire flared up, hot and consuming. He seemed to know exactly how she wanted to be touched, his lips and teeth answering every unspoken command, every silent entreaty.

She let him push her gently backwards on to the bed, surrendering her body to his passion. There was no sense of familiarity, no sense of repetition, even though they had made love more than once before. It was a voyage into a wonderful new world of experience and sensation. She wondered dizzily whether she would ever tire of their lovemaking... whether he would ever have enough of her.

Not to judge by the way he was devouring her with kisses, caressing the satin of her skin, sucking her into a spinning whirlpool of passion!

'Kirby, my darling,' he said, his voice ragged, 'you're my life, my soul. You know I can't live without you. Tell me you feel the same way!'

'You know how I feel,' she responded in a shaking whisper. 'You've always known how I felt, Damian.'

'We've spent so long apart...' he paused to haul off his shirt, revealing the tanned magnificence of his torso '... we're not going to spend a second apart ever again.'

'Oh, darling, we can't—not here!'

'Why not?' he demanded, coming to her again.

'Because it's not ours... not yet!'

'If you want it, it's yours, Kirby. I put down a deposit this morning, before I came to the Lodge. I know I should have consulted you, but I was terrified someone else would buy it first.'

'And you were anticipating a long siege?' She smiled up into his dazzling eyes.

'As long as it took.'

She ran her hands over his skin, tracing the muscles of his chest, the lithe waist and taut, flat stomach. 'And do you really want me—little Kirby Bryant? You once thought I was too immature for you, Damian.'

'Not any more,' he said, his mouth roaming hungrily over her breasts. She felt his tongue encircle her swollen nipples, making her shudder with pleasure. '*I* was the one who was immature, Kirby. Now I know exactly what I want. And I want only you.'

She closed her eyes, lost in the closeness of him. Mrs Kirby Holt. She remembered how often she had thought those words, long ago, never really believing they could come true. And now they were real, within her grasp. The impossible had happened, and joy could be hers. All she had to do was reach out and touch it.

'I love you, Damian,' she said quietly. 'I've always loved you, with all my heart and soul. You were always the centre of my life. The most wonderful thing that ever happened to me. I only have one real wish, and that's to make you as happy as I know how, for the rest of our lives together.'

'Then you'll marry me?' he asked, looking down at her with brilliant eyes.

'Yes,' she nodded. 'Tomorrow, if you want.'

'Oh, yes. That's what I want, Kirby.'

Then there was only the need they felt for one another, the consuming hunger which wrapped their hearts in flame. Kirby had never loved any man like this, had never wanted any man the way she wanted Damian now. As he took her body in his arms, she felt her soul soar like an eagle, with his by its side, high into the immense darkness of space.

'If there's no further business,' Damian said, 'I leave the final word to the chair.'

'Thank you,' Kirby nodded. She looked around the boardroom. She was wearing one of her most formal suits, a charcoal costume with a white blouse and black court shoes. It could not make her soft beauty any more severe, but it was certainly businesslike.

The faces around the long, polished table were all smiling in contentment. It had probably been the most eventful and at the same time the most satisfactory board meeting in the history of Waterford Electronics. Her eyes lifted to the portrait of Keith that she had had moved from the main office so that it would from now on smile gently down on to the boardroom. Well, I did it, Keith, she told him silently. I've preserved the company as you would have wanted it.

Then she took a deep breath. 'As outgoing chairman of Waterford Electronics,' she began, 'I am confident of leaving the firm in the best possible hands. I mean that in three senses. Firstly, I think we ought to congratulate ourselves on acquiring our new chairman of the board—Mr Roderick Braithwaite. He has been an exceptional manager for several years, and we all know that the firm will go from strength to strength under his chairmanship.'

There was a scattering of applause, and Roderick beamed around him, accepting handshakes and pats on the back from all sides. He had got what he wanted at last. And, with the new plans for expansion and a more dynamic marketing policy already on the drawing-board, Roderick Braithwaite was one of the happiest men in Yorkshire today.

'Secondly,' she went on, 'we can also be confident that my late husband's spirit of altruism will not be lost. We've approved the new constitution which commits Waterford Electronics to helping the community in the future, just as it has done in the past. I'm delighted to say that there is even a programme to increase charitable work over the next couple of years, as the profits increase.'

She met Damian's slate-blue eyes. They were amused, tender, loving—even though his face was expressionless. She had to fight down her own loving smile in reply.

'Thirdly, and most importantly,' she concluded, 'we should congratulate the Holt Corporation, in the form of its head, Mr Damian Holt, who are now the major shareholders and new owners of the firm.' She waited for the applause to die down. 'I think I can safely say that every single member of this board welcomes the fact that we are now part of the large and successful family of companies under the Holt Corporation umbrella. We welcome the protection and support that implies... and we look forward to a relationship of unbroken success with our new parent company. The integrity of Mr Holt himself is our best guarantee that Waterford Electronics will be run in a just and fair manner. Thank you all.'

The board meeting broke up in an atmosphere of jollity and good humour. Kirby found herself the centre of a group of board members, all wanting to shake her hand, and to congratulate her on the news.

'You've been an absolutely splendid chairman,' an elderly man was beaming. 'We'll miss you badly. But you've steered Waterford Electronics into a magnificent position. Don't know how you did it, my dear, but well done!'

She could see Damian at the other end of the room, and Roderick in the middle, both also the centres of similarly attentive groups. It took almost an hour to accept all the good wishes, and extricate herself from various invitations.

At last she was leaving the boardroom with an escort of attentive males. Leaving it, she suddenly realised, for the last time. She walked through the office, looking around, and thinking back over the past year, as she listened with one ear to the conversation all around her.

Outside, in the car park, the sun shone down brilliantly. It was one of those rare, lovely, crisp winter days, with a dazzling blue sky overhead.

She felt as though she were in a dream. A dream of happiness, of achievement.

She said goodbye to various people. Watched various people say goodbye to one another. Saw them get into their cars and drive away into the afternoon.

And then she was standing there alone, dreamily soaking up the sun. She felt as mountain climbers must feel as they reached the peaks they'd fought so hard to attain. A sensation of having broken through the clouds, of having left all unhappiness, all disappointment behind her for ever. It was love that gave her that feeling. The love that Damian filled her with, brimming her spirit.

She felt the shiver of memory cross her skin as she thought back over these past days of lovemaking. How he'd used his flawless, magnificent body to exalt her, to bring her to the heights of response, again and again and again.

But it was so very much more than just sex. It was something that made them one person, whole and indivisible. The most wonderful feeling she had ever known. That they were growing hourly ever more expert at knowing one another's pleasures, that they could never put out the flames of desire that were constantly springing up between them... all that was wonderful.

More wonderful was the sure knowledge that they were equally matched in spirit. The knowledge that told her their marriage, their life together, was going to be immaculately happy...

She felt his presence at her side, and turned to smile up into his face.

'Need a lift home, Mrs Waterford?'

'Why, thank you, Mr Holt.'

He gave her his arm, and they walked together to his car. 'Thank you for those kind words back there, by the way,' he said solemnly. 'Much obliged.'

'A good morning's work all round,' she agreed. 'Well, Mr Holt. It seems you own my company.'

'And it seems, Mrs Waterford, that you own my heart.' She couldn't stop herself from smiling. 'Not to mention a large portion of your money. What am I going to do with it all?'

'Blow it on diamonds,' he suggested, opening the door of the Porsche. 'Give it to the poor. Use it to buy Old Master paintings. Or a racehorse. Or a hospital in India.'

'I might do all those things,' she nodded. 'You're a mine of good ideas, Mr Holt.'

As they drove out of the factory gates, she laid her curly head on his shoulder, and sighed.

'That,' he judged, 'is the sigh of a truly happy woman.'

'If you only knew how I felt, Damian. I feel so—*free*. As if a gigantic weight has been lifted off my shoulders. I could fly away like a kite.'

'Except I'll always be holding your string,' he smiled. 'Oh, by the way—I've spoken to the vicar. We've set the date for the wedding on the eighteenth of next month.'

'Without consulting *me*?' she exclaimed, sitting up indignantly. 'Now look here, mister! You may have bought out Waterford Electronics, and you may have conquered my heart—but my mind is still very much my own, thank you very much!'

He laughed helplessly at her expression. 'Have you any objection to the eighteenth?'

'Of course not.'

'Then shut up,' he advised.

'You do know that the marriage service has changed,' she said significantly. 'It doesn't read, "Love, honour and obey," any more. Just, "Love, honour and cherish." Nobody says *obey* any more.'

'You are,' he informed her silkily. 'You're going to say the old words.'

'I am not!'

'Oh, yes, you are. Or the whole thing is off!'

'You don't scare me,' she snorted. 'You tried to shrug me off once before—and look where it got you.'

'"Love, honour and obey,"' he said.

'"Love, honour and *cherish*."'

They were still wrangling about it as they pulled up in front of Ely Hall a quarter of an hour later.

They got out of the car, and both looked at the enchanted old place. Its venerable stones seemed to smile a welcome at them. The mullioned windows were like friendly eyes, staring serenely out over the wonderful future that stretched ahead for them.

The front door was open. The furniture van on the gravel outside was unloading some of Kirby's things from the Lodge. Not a great deal...she was selling most of the contents with the house. Leaving her old life behind her to take up the new.

Or, at least, some of her old life; they caught sight of Mrs Carstairs instructing the removals men where to take things.

'All right,' she sighed, taking Damian's hand. '"Obey", it is.'

'I've changed my mind. We'll have "cherish".'

They looked at one another, and smiled. 'It's the same thing,' Kirby said.

'Yes,' he agreed.

They kissed, with the tender love she knew they would always have. And then they walked forward together into their new life.

Calloway Corners

In September, Harlequin is proud to bring readers four
involving, romantic stories about the Calloway sisters,
set in Calloway Corners, Louisiana. Written by four of
Harlequin's most popular and award-winning authors,
you'll be enchanted by these sisters and the men
they love!

MARIAH by Sandra Canfield
JO by Tracy Hughes
TESS by Katherine Burton
EDEN by Penny Richards

As an added bonus, you can enter a sweepstakes contest
to win a trip to Calloway Corners, and meet all four
authors. Watch for details in all Calloway Corners books
in September.

CAL93

HARLEQUIN ✦ PRESENTS®

A Year
DOWN UNDER

In 1993, Harlequin Presents celebrates the land down under. In October, let us take you to rural New Zealand in WINTER OF DREAMS by Susan Napier, Harlequin Presents # 1595.

Olivia Marlow never wants to see Jordan Pendragon again—their first meeting had been a humiliating experience. The sexy New Zealander had rejected her then, but now he seems determined to pursue her. Olivia knows she must tread carefully—she has something to hide. But then, it's equally obvious that Jordan has his own secret....

Share the adventure—and the romance—of A Year Down Under!

Available this month in
A YEAR DOWN UNDER

AND THEN CAME MORNING
by Daphne Clair
Harlequin Presents # 1586
Available wherever Harlequin books are sold.

YDU-S